To Janet

Have a good
read

Olga

CHECKERBERRY

BY

OLGA BEATTY

CHECKERBERRY

ISBN 1 85863 027 4

First Published 1993 by

MINERVA PRESS
2, Old Brompton Road,
London SW7 3DQ.

Printed in Great Britain by
B.W.D. Ltd. Northolt, Middlesex.

CHECKERBERRY

"Damn! Damn! Damn! Damn! Da..! "

"...and who, in the name of God, are you?".

The broad Irish brogue startled her in mid-damn; she turned and was confronted by a man with a devilish glint in his eye, unpolished brawny looks that only just escaped plainness - but there was something about him that caused her heart to flutter. An embarrassed flush ran the full length of her face down into her neck. "I'm - I'm Jill, the new school teacher".

His voice betrayed a tone of mirth. "A school mistress! Well, I'll be damned! I sure as hell am glad it's not me taking the brunt of all that damnin'. Nice to meet you, Jill", he held out his hand to her, "Bid goodbye to the man you're damnin' and hello to Patrick O'Rafferty".

*****

Olga Beatty, 5th child in a family of eight, was born and brought up in Omagh, County Tyrone. While juggling the demands of a family of four with assisting her eldest son in running a wine importing business she went back to colle ge in Teesside and was encouraged by her English tutor to take up writing. When life became less hectic she decided to give it a try.

She now lives in Cambridge.

"Think of the devil!"
"God Almighty, think of going to sleep".
"That's it - 'God Almighty, think of the devil'".

To my husband who put up with my active mind in the middle of the night while I was writing this book.

Ian Beatty

Exceedingly rare is the artist of whom we can say 'was truly supreme'. I say it of you -

Bernard Shore

Not only was he a leading viola player but he was also an accomplished writer, gifted with shrewdness and wit. Having read his book, 'The Orchestra Speaks', published 1938, enabled me to hone into the wonderful world of classical music, thereby making my book Checkerberry possible.

Chapter One

Jill was on edge all day at the thought of her impending interview with Sir Malcolm Saunders, Chairman of the Bank. When she arrived at her desk this morning, Miss Foster, the Chairman's personal secretary, handed her a memo.

"Why Sir Malcolm wishes to be inconvenienced by seeing you personally, I have no idea. He is a very busy man; I would suggest you arrive a few minutes early for the appointment and announce yourself as I will already have left".

She probably knows I'm for the chop, Jill had thought, watching her move off in an egotistical fashion, nose in the air. Miss Foster hardly ever smiled; her face might crack. She was a real goody-goody type who very likely never uttered a swear word in her life and wore the same type of clothes every day; a starched white blouse with pearls hung neatly around the collar and a pleated black skirt.

The memo was short and to the point - simply requesting Jill to see the Chairman in his office at 5.35pm.

There was an unprecedented shake-out in the finance industry and half of the jobs were to go here over the next two years. Why should she, a raw recruit, expect to be kept on? Redundancies were usually dealt with by the Personnel Department but for the life of her Jill couldn't think of anything else she would have been summoned for; therefore she prepared herself for the worst.

Her heart was hammering as she knocked on his office door. Stepping inside and trying to keep her voice on an even keel, she said, "You wished to see me, Sir Malcolm!".

Sir Malcolm, a very popular Chairman, in his early sixties, stood up and greeted her courteously. He was dignified without being pompous and his voice had a sonorous quality, "I am very pleased to see you, Miss Ashton and I apologise for keeping you late, but I was tied up in meetings all day".

With a flick of his hand he gestured to a seat and sat himself down to face her in his elaborate swivel chair. He picked up a document and waved it in front of her. "I have read through your CV with interest. I see you hold a qualified teacher's diploma and before joining our bank, six months ago, you had two year's experience in teaching five to seven year old children.

"It may seem strange coming from me but would you be interested in a private teaching position in the South West of Ireland?".

Jill was flabbergasted. She was being offered a job when all day she had been contemplating getting the sack. She had left her teaching post in Devon nine months ago, for the love of a man who had since rejected her. Maria, her friend, recommended her for this job in the bank and she was lucky to get it. It paid the rent while she waited for a teaching vacancy to emerge, preferably as far away as possible, at the agency where she was registered. Ireland wasn't a place she knew anything about, other than thatched cottages, rain and peat bogs, but she had no ties now that he had - Damn him!

Sir Malcolm's voice broke into her thoughts, he had taken off his glasses and was waving them about. "One would have to be a nature lover and maybe a bit of a recluse to accept this position on offer, as Checkerberry is very secluded, but there are countless advantages for the right person. I have probably sprung this on you but are you even slightly interested, Miss Ashton?"

She clutched her handbag with both hands tensely. Although demanding, it would be a challenge and it would get her out of London; it was vital that she got away. She had been applying for jobs in other countries for ages but to no avail. Jill looked at him with wide, keen eyes and spoke positively, "I am interested in knowing more about the position".

Sir Malcolm, who had been fingering his fountain pen nervously, said in a relieved voice, "Good! The children are orphans, three boys and one girl. Two of the boys are twins aged eight, the other boy is six and the little girl under four. Their parents, my daughter and her husband, were killed in an aeroplane crash while they were on their way to Zurich six months ago. The three older children had already started school but one of them is proving somewhat of a problem so I have decided to have them educated privately, at home, for the time being, that is, until I can assess the situation further.

"I know that does not sound a very permanent basis for the person taking on this venture, but there will be a salary written into the contract should the job fall through within a year. In your case, however, if you decide to take on the job and we find that being sent to a proper school would be in the children's best interest, there will be a guaranteed place kept here for you in the bank as well as the one year's salary".

Jill felt a rush of pity for Sir Malcolm as she suddenly remembered Maria telling her about how the news of the plane crash had gone round the office. Very soon after that sad event Jill got the job with the bank, but like all sad events it was soon forgotten about. Only the senior management would have known that Sir Malcolm had taken on the responsibility for the children's welfare.

"I was very sorry to hear of your daughter and son-in-law's unfortunate death and subject to the children liking me, I would be pleased to be considered for the post", said Jill with sincerity.

Sir Malcolm hurriedly came around the desk with his hand outstretched, saying, "I have considered you, my dear. I wish to offer you the post. You see, you have been very highly recommended by a very prestigious man and a close friend of mine".

He took Jill's hand in a firm clasp and shook it vigorously.

"May I enquire who recommended me?", asked Jill politely.

"Dr Barry Thorpe, the composer", answered Sir Malcolm,

"We have been family friends for many years. His father and I were best friends when boys, he and his dear wife have sadly passed on".

Jill was taken aback and wished she had heard who had recommended her before she had accepted the post, as the worst possible situation she could imagine herself in was to be indebted to Barry Thorpe.

Sir Malcolm was speaking, she tried to concentrate on his words, "There will be no need to work out your notice, I will have it recorded in your personnel file that you have been granted sabbatical leave". He stopped speaking and looked at her anxiously. Her tenseness was communicative.

"Have you any problems, Miss Ashton? You are not having second thoughts about the post".

She wasn't going to pass over this job simply because he had recommended her, nor had she any intention of ever thanking him for putting the opportunity of it her way. "No, Sir Malcolm", she said with clarity, "I am just a little over-awed by it all, I am honoured to have been offered the assignment and hopefully I will make a success of it".

Jill sat next to Sir Malcolm on the private plane on their way to Skibbereen, western Cork. She found him a particularly pleasant man. The subordinate staff at her level rarely got to meet the Chairman, but he was liked among her superiors and it was well known that he put a lot of effort into creating a contented working environment for all levels of employees. Even now he was quizzing her about her colleagues and if there were any improvements that could be made towards that end. He spoke little of the children, but gave her background information on the general area.

"Skibbereen is the hub of the day-to-day business of western Cork; it is a town where the colour combinations are unrestrained, going on reckless. It is the focal point of the thriving agricultural community and the beautiful secluded area, which includes nearby Ballydehob, attracts a talented collection of artists, sculptors and writers from as far afield as France and Germany.

"The Checkerberry estate is isolated, one could go for weeks without seeing a soul".

The views were breathtaking as the plane made its decent over the southern coast of Ireland. There was a patchwork of small fields in varying shades of green and an abundance of lakes. The pilot made a special deviation for Jill's benefit so that she could admire the vast amount of rocky hills, vertical cliffs and beautiful old castles.

They drew closer in their approach to land on the outskirts of Skibbereen and Jill realised why one would have to enjoy being a recluse as the Georgian splendour, secluded and elegant, was set in acres upon acres of green fields and woodland with no sign of any other occupation in sight for miles. Looking down she knew intuitively that she would be happy retreating into a world of her own and begin a new life as a hermit with only her young wards to keep her company. As the plane touched the runway with a bump she became excited at the thought of the solitude in the heart of the countryside.

The pilot gave them a helping hand to disembark, loaded their baggage onto the waiting jeep and shook hands before taking off again.

The long path leading from the runway to the house was flanked on each side by meadows of dazzling wild flowers, colourful poppies, cornflowers and marigolds. As they drove nearer the more elaborate the grounds became, the shrubbery and flower beds all blending in magnificently.

A very elegant, slim lady in her fifties appeared at the front entrance to meet them as they pulled up and Sir Malcolm introduced her as Sylvia, his wife.

"I am very pleased to make your acquaintance and welcome you to Checkerberry", said Lady Sylvia as she offered Jill a well manicured hand. Her eyes ran over Jill approvingly observing her neat appearance. "Let's enjoy a nice cup of tea inside while the little terrors are out with Michelle, their nanny".

She stepped aside gesturing Jill to proceed into the splendid neo-classical hallway.

Sir Malcolm seemed to acquire a different personality now that the grandiloquence and pressures of the bank had temporarily fallen from his shoulders. "Don't forget your delicious shortcake biscuits, Jane", he called to the housekeeper in the kitchen.

Jane, a small woman with fine modelled features and neatly permed steel grey hair, hurriedly appeared round the door and shook hands with Jill, saying, "I'm so delighted you're here, Miss Ashton, maybe now we will get some peace from those boisterous youngsters".

"Oh, Jane, don't frighten her off", quipped Sir Malcolm. "They are quite good really - when they are asleep that is".

Jill followed them both into a restful and bright room overlooking a well stocked garden. Two adorable cream with blue points Persian cats lay sprawled on the back of one of the seats. The larger of the two jumped down and purred at Jill and she swiftly reached down and stroked it.

"Luckily Milly and Maxie have wonderful temperaments as Bonny has almost mauled them to death", said Lady Sylvia.

While they were having tea Sir Malcolm put an awkward question her way when he asked, "Why did you leave your teaching post in Devon, Jill?".

She hesitated slightly and fidgeted with her necklace before speaking, "My friends had moved away taking my social life with them. I've got it out of my system now and I do feel passionately about the countryside - to my cost, I found big city life wasn't for me".

Sir Malcolm and Lady Sylvia observed it had been a

delicate question.

Jane showed Jill over the house in order to familiarise her with it as it was to be her work place and home. The Georgian house with Edwardian additions had been sympathetically restored whilst retaining the original features.

The country kitchen had an old range, a stone-flagged floor and antique furniture right down to the copper pans hanging on the wall. The living rooms each had unique colour co-ordination that carried through to the smallest detail. There was a magnificent drawing room, elegantly furnished. The extensive basement consisted of a table tennis room, music room and a large room set aside as the classroom.

Sir Malcolm's office was fitted out with the latest communication technology to keep him in touch with his head office in London.

Jill was allocated an en-suite bedroom with modern fitted furniture. After bouncing on the bed to test if it was as comfortable as it looked she set about unpacking enthusiastically. She heard the children noisily arrive and tentatively made her way downstairs.

Everyone accumulated in the hall and Lady Sylvia tried to keep order till the introductions were made.

The pretty nanny stepped forward, shook Jill by the hand and smiled as she said, "I'm Michelle Edgar, nanny and peace maker".

She then restrained the little girl with the beautiful shining black hair from pushing forward by saying, "No! Not your turn yet, eldest first". The little girl lowered her big brown eyes then sidled over to Sir Malcolm and clung to his trousered leg, while he patted her head consolingly.

Michelle introduced Iain and Alan, eight year old twins. They each stepped forward to shake hands in turn. They were not identical but resembled each other, Iain being slightly shorter than Alan. She then introduced Jamie, six, who seemed extremely shy and shook hands only when coaxed. When Bonny was introduced she handed Jill a bunch of drooping daisies and she responded with, "Oh, how lovely! Thank you very much, these shall be our very first bunch of flowers for the classroom".

Sir Malcolm and Lady Sylvia, seemed happy and relieved that first impressions all round seemed promising.

In the early evening Jill wandered through the divine grounds - she came upon the aromatic herb garden, an enchanting retreat - she could sense a certain something in the atmosphere, it seemed fresher, sweeter, wilder yet welcoming. The many superb herbaceous perennials noted for their striking foliage were braided with small leafed ferns that shivered in the breeze, lending a soft feathery touch among the huge rhubarb-like platters. The variety of the textures and colours played an important role in creating a unique scene.

Beyond a stone wall, overgrown with sweet pea, she came upon an abundance of mature trees and semi-tropical rare shrubs with a fast flowing stream meandering through the lot.

She stood gazing into the clear running water, watching it rush over the jagged stones in a fast current. She had fled across the sea to Ireland to get away from everything that reminded her of him; his face staring at her as she flicked through magazines; from the covers of records and from posters advertising his next appearance as she glided up the elevator in the underground. Lo and behold he had gone far beyond the usual bounds of reverie and was manifesting himself in the form of the stream:

"He is as a fast flowing stream;
Dam him! Dam him! Dam him! Damn!   Damn! Damn!
Damn! Damn! Da..!'

"...and who, in the name of God, are you?".

The broad Irish brogue startled her in mid-damn; she turned and was confronted by a man with a devilish glint in his eye, unpolished brawny looks that only just escaped plainness - but there was something about him that caused her heart to flutter. An embarrassed flush ran the full length of her face down into her neck. "I'm... I'm Jill, the new school teacher".

His voice betrayed a tone of mirth. "A school mistress! Well, I'll be damned! I sure as hell am glad it's not me taking the brunt of all that damnin'. Nice to meet you, Jill", he held out his hand to her, "Bid goodbye to the man you're damnin' and hello to Patrick O'Rafferty".

Chapter Two

Next day Jill and Sir Malcolm went off to explore what local material was available to them in the line of educational aids, literature and books, so that the children would not fall short on anything. They came back tired and overladen.

The walls of the classroom had been freshly painted in cream. Perhaps later, Jill would organize the children to carry out floral and wild life stencilling, after practising on sheets of paper. It would need nothing further at this stage as they would gradually add pieces of interest and work displays.

Sir Malcolm and Lady Sylvia, gardener, nanny, housekeeper and children all assisted her in organising the classroom. Furniture needed moved around and teaching aids left handy so that the children could work on the planned activities with maximum ease. Displays had to be set up, to give the younger children things to look at, handle and talk about in relation to the work that was planned. It was important to make the physical organization of the classroom work for her rather than against her.

A few days later the light plane was sitting on the runway in readiness for take off. Sir Malcolm and Lady Sylvia were going back to London. As they got into the jeep Sir Malcolm said, "I wish you all the best, Jill, but if there are any problems you know how to reach me, I can't guarantee that I would be in a position to drop all and come back but Lady Sylvia certainly would".

They all watched as the plane took off and waved until it disappeared from view.

"It is the first time that Lady Sylvia has felt relaxed enough to accompany Sir Malcolm to London since the children's parents died. The superb flat they own in London is luxurious and I know Lady Sylvia would spend more time there if she could". said Jane to Jill as they followed Michelle and the children.

"It has been a heavy responsibility for them at their age", Jill said sadly.

"Oh! Don't mention it", said Jane, "It's almost beyond them but they do their best".

There was only one day left for preparation as she had planned for the children to start school tomorrow with the exception of Bonny who would attend for three hours only each day.

Jill knew she was taking on a hefty responsibility and that the first few days could be nerve wrecking, indeed chaotic, until she had established routines that matched her style and that of her new charges. The twins would already have routines so she would have to introduce new ways of working. Although the Irish Government laid down educational guidelines, she would have to make up her own curriculum and classroom management - there would be no inspector or head teacher to supervise, advise and offer help. Then of course exam papers had to be generated relating to the syllabus. She would also have to plan day trips and other forms of excitement; maintain a balance between developing her own capacities and contributions; assess the children's development and match work to their needs.

As she lay in bed that night, tired but sleep eluding her, the haunting started again as usual. Her body vibrated and ached futilely with a desperate longing for his virile and passionate body. She closed her weary eyes in anguish and prayed that God would rid her of this erotomania that had engulfed her mind and body for so long.

Chapter Three

The weeks that followed were demanding but rewarding as she took the children, each at their different stages, through the course of study she had set for them. Fortunately none of them seemed to have severe behavioural problems due to the cruel deprivation of losing their parents; they were resilient and well adjusted children, eagerly falling in with Jill's new routines.

She monitored the progress of each child individually observing how their minds worked and decided what help they needed. Alan seemed to have got over his tantrums and the psychotherapist was no longer needed but he found it difficult to remember a new word from one page to the next, while his twin Iain, soaked it up like blotting paper but had a low boredom threshold and constantly needed new challenges. Jamie was quiet and because he was no trouble tended to merge into the background and could easily be overlooked. Bonny was a delight and a proper little chatterbox. She had just discovered the little, but powerful, word 'and'; she could happily talk all day fastening one sentence onto another.

Joseph McCrory, a very talented music teacher, slightly built and with a happy disposition, came twice a week to give the children music lessons. Jill was glad about that arrangement as she didn't feel qualified enough to teach music. The only instrument she was in any way competent on was the flute.

Jill and Michelle became good friends, not only did they resemble each other in looks, they had a lot in common and the children's best interest at heart. They both agreed that working with children wasn't always a bed of roses, but on a good day it beats anything else you can think of. Michelle was full of admiration for Jill's achievement and congratulated her on the marvellous way she had coped single handed with the unfamiliar situation in hand and Jill answered, "I suppose I have to thank being an only child for my ability to come up with good ideas, I had to think for myself. Being an only child isn't all good though, I missed the natural rivalry which is healthy, the sharing and confiding".

Michelle made no bones of the fact, that although she was happy working here for the present, her special preference was to work with babies. She was a fully qualified nursery nurse, patient and imaginative, with an abundance of common sense thrown in for good measure.

Her boyfriend, Patrick O'Rafferty, who startled the life out of Jill on her first day, when he went to the stream thinking he saw Michelle, owned an expanding wine importing business in the nearby town of Bantry, had humorously said that if it was a baby she wanted, he would give her one, she only had to lie back, open her legs and think of The Emerald Isle.

Patrick, big in character but by no means tall, on the stocky side with mousy hair that flopped onto his cheek and just a shade too long at the back so it curled up at the neck. His looks wouldn't stand out in a crowd but the more one saw of him the more attractive he seemed to become. He was one of the outstanding personalities of the wine trade and enjoyed close contacts with Europe.

His deep knowledge of wine, his warmth and ready humour made him a favourite with wine merchants around the country and he had established a reputation for expertise in his field. Like all other small businesses the recession was hitting him deep, but he had all the attributes of becoming a prosperous businessman.

He had Jill bowled over by his immense charm from the first minute she put her hand in his - she liked him and his drawling Irish twang. Although even-tempered he was outwardly gregarious and good fun and each time he called to collect Michelle, he had them all in stitches of laughter with his lighthearted banter and interminable assortment of, funny and mostly risqué jokes. His whole being seemed to buzz and hum with vitality and energy; he was forever grabbing Jill from behind, prattling, "How is the gorgeous, curvaceous Jill today?", then he would swing her off her feet.

'Patrick O'Rafferty, you must have been a devil of a little boy, your mother's heart must have been broken with your pranks'. Jill would screech something to that effect, releasing herself from his tight grip.

Tonight it was Jane's turn to be teased. "You're looking very sexy tonight, Jane, pity I couldn't keep old John sober long enough to come with me and take you out on the town for a few jars".

"Off with you before I whack you one", yelled Jane.

Michelle dragged him off but he simply had to have the last word, "Now, Jane, don't get your knickers in a twist".

When they drove off Jane turned to Jill and said, "It would do you good to find yourself a young man and go out and sample the night life, it's not right for such a pretty young girl to be cooped up here night after night with an old fogey like me".

Jill answered lightly, "Ah! Maybe when I'm old and in my thirties I'll look for a husband for myself, but in the meantime I'm happy to remain footloose and fancy free. I've had enough commitment to that particular gender to last me a long time. As for night life, livelier souls might wish for that, I've never hankered after it".

Jane, in her wisdom, knew only too well that the words harboured a severe hurt and wished she could get her hands on the scoundrel. She wouldn't wish on anybody what happened to herself years ago. Here she was, an old maid, because one scoundrel led her up the garden path.

Jill settled in front of the fire and started knitting where she had left off the previous night. She was working on a little green and blue stripped jumper for Jamie and was going to surprise him with it on their day out next week.

Jane read poetry in the evenings between nodding off. Her job was tiring but it was a labour of love and as long as they were willing to employ her, she was willing to work - well for a year or so anyway.

It was during these nights together that Jill learnt about the children's family.

Teresa, Sir Malcolm's daughter, had been married to Geoff Webb, a doctor in general practice. Jane had been with them in this house from the very beginning. They were married five years before giving birth to the twins. The others followed in steps of stairs. They were very much in love and when they were here this had been a very happy home.

At the fateful time of the air crash, Geoff was to attend a medical conference in Switzerland and Sir Malcolm and Lady Sylvia encouraged Teresa to take the break as well. It was the one and only occasion that they had left the children and everyone had been completely devastated by the disaster. The children, although buffeted, seemed to cope better than the grown ups and luckily, with much love and devotion, came through relatively unscathed.

Sir Malcolm had been knighted eight years ago. He and Lady Sylvia had owned a large country estate in Worthing but sold up and moved here straight after the misfortune. They love this place and the people around are friendly but they also miss the life they had been used to previously; he had been looking forward to retirement and enjoying the pursuits of a country gentleman. As it is he will work out his time in the bank, probably spend a lot of time at their London flat then retire here.

After a hot milky drink Jill bid Jane goodnight and said she would look in on the children on the way to her room. She tucked each one of them in and felt sad when she thought of the many times Teresa must have lovingly performed this duty. She lingered with the sleeping Jamie, his light brown hair, streaked blond with the sun, had fallen over his eyes. Leaning over she gently moved it back then kissed his forehead.

Time passed quickly, weeks turned into months. Her obsession with him was fading slowly but surely; she could walk by the stream without being paranoid in feeling the need to dam it; it still reminded her of him, but she wanted it to flow away from her and disperse into the sea. As she lay in bed at night, he was now a fleeting thought, not a craving.

Sir Malcolm and Lady Sylvia made a point of visiting one weekend each month and the children looked forward eagerly to these visits. They both marvelled at Jill's achievements; praised her constantly for her dedication, devotion, love and sacrifice. She waved it all away as if it was nothing.

On the last occasion they were here the children stood before them in the classroom and rattled off an old farmer's toast to the trees in the orchard, in the Devonshire language rather than dialect.

Here's to thee, old apple tree
Whence thou may'st bud
And whence thou may'st blow
And whence thou may'st bear
Apples enow;
Hats full! Caps full!
Bushel, bushel, sacks full!
And my pockets full too!
Huzza!

Bonny yelled three Huzzas, as she liked the way Jill had taught them to call it out.

The children were remarkably content to bid them goodbye at the end of each visit, chanting happily in unison, "Goodbye, Grandma - Goodbye, Grandpa".

Jill made a point of reading an Enid Blyton story on the Monday mornings when their grandparents left, simply to cheer them up, although more often than not, Grandma and Grandpa were forgotten before they reached their desks.

"I can't remember if it was 'Poor Captain Puss' or 'The Elephant and the Snail' that we got up to last time", said Jill, in the pretence that they had one up on her in memory.

They all shrieked "The Elephant and the Snail", zealously.

"Once upon a time...". She had a knack for story telling and the children weren't averse to hearing the animal stories several times. Being imaginative in making facial expressions and animal sounds she adopted a pace and pitch to gain maximum effect.

The children spent lunchtimes with Michelle and Jane. That was Jill's time to assess and analyze as she nibbled her sandwiches. She sometimes worried if she was really making the children think. Am I picking up their trend of thought or simply imposing my own on them? Are my explanations making sense? She listened to tape recordings of previous lessons, heard her own voice through the

children's ears and realized the thinking behind their
words. She was learning while teaching and thoroughly
enjoying it.

Although, on the whole, most days ran reasonably
smoothly, some were tiresome and it was on one of those
harrowing days when Bonny wet her pants and Jamie cut
his knee simultaneously, that Barry arrived on the scene.
Jamie needed a cuddle for a minute to get over the shock
of his bleeding knee while Bonny stood with her legs apart
screaming for dry pants.

"Where are her dry pants?", a voice hollered and they all
turned round in amazement.

"In there!", said Jill shocked, while nodding to the
cupboard.

He took out the first pair of pants at hand, which were
boy's, pulled off Bonny's wet ones and replaced them
with the dry pair.

The older boys gave him time to complete the job before
throwing themselves at him to be hugged one by one. The
class was completely out of control in the excitement of
his arrival. "Uncle Barry! Do you like our teacher? She
tells super stories!", said Jamie, his cut knee forgotten.

Barry's eyes shone with a look usually reserved for only
those who were really special. He spoke to each child in
turn, giving them equal attention, then walked to the door
and called Michelle to come and take them for half an
hour while he had a word with Jill.

Jill was fuming when the door closed behind them, "What right have you to come in here and disrupt my routine?", she shrieked angrily.

"Calm down! It didn't look much of a routine to me, or are wet pants and cut knees the order of the day?", he retorted smugly.

How dare he! She felt angry enough to hit him or if there had been a gun handy she would have been tempted to shoot him in a very delicate place. Instead, for the first time in her career, she felt beaten and her credibility was further damaged when the tears started running down her face - it was just too much to endure having him there, suddenly occupying her space, just when the terrible emotional torment was beginning to fade to a tolerable level. The last time she had set eyes on him was when she lay beneath him in bed. She knew it looked really bad as he towered above her observing her lack of control.

He softened and said, "Alright, I don't expect you to be a paragon all of the time".

That didn't help and she cried more. Then he said, "Jill, I am not accusing you of incompetence for Christ's sake; if anyone knows how you can control a class, its me. Remember, I stood and watched in awe that day when you silenced a whispering library with just a lift of your eyebrow".

She sniffled as she tried to gain command and met his gaze, "Why are you here?", she asked defiantly.

His gaze slowly moved to her full, naturally pink, trembling lips then met her eyes again quickly as he answered, "To take Iain and Alan fishing perhaps and see how they are all getting along with the music teacher I engaged for them. I shall be here for a week or two".

Jill couldn't believe her ears; she would have to go away if he stayed here. He obviously had no moral dilemma about what had happened between them and not only that, with him around she would feel as if he was assessing her all the time. "Have you asked Sir Malcolm's permission to disrupt the children and the whole household?", she asked with ill-disguised contempt.

"I don't need Sir Malcolm's permission, I had an open invitation from Geoff and Teresa; it still stands".

He walked to the door and turning the handle he said, "Don't worry, I will keep out of your way as much as possible".

As she stared at the closed door, she knew he certainly would do that; it was the one thing he was expert at, even though he knew she worshipped the ground he walked upon and had longed for his touch.

She wished she hadn't felt the way she did that night and blushed at the thought of her frenzied need of him. She also wished she had been superhuman and when he put the damned question to her, in that hoarse and sexy voice of his, she had answered him simply, 'No!'. Oh, how she would just have loved to have left him totally and absolutely frustrated.

With a shrug of her shoulders she thanked God, that with her new life and the help of prayer, the crazy obsession was almost behind her now. Yes! The demented insanity, her mother's words, was fading at last.

Jill and Michelle helped each other out with the children whenever possible, tonight Jill took it upon herself to help bath them. The older boys liked to shower while the younger two loved splashing and playing in the bath. They had so many floating toys in the bath that they were hardly visible themselves.

They were both physically exhausted after they had the children, chased, caught, dried, dressed, storied and kissed goodnight.

"How often does Barry come here?", asked Jill as they retired to Michelle's room for a girlie chat.

"Not as often as we would all like", replied Michelle, "The place livens up when he arrives, the children adore him and he likewise. He has been away for some months at concerts and receptions in Florence, Naples and Rome and we have all missed his regular visits".

"Sir Malcolm told me that he is a long time friend of the entire family, also about how closely he grew up with Teresa and that they were more like brother and sister. Did he become good friends with Geoff as well?".

"Oh yes! He actually introduced them and was over the moon when they clicked. I've been here only a year, but

Jane said that if Geoff hadn't approved of Barry's presence around the place then Teresa probably wouldn't have married him and that would have been sad as they were madly in love and suited each other down to the ground. But of course there was never any question of that, indeed Geoff and he became even closer as buddies".

Jill had become increasingly gloomy at the prospect of his stay; she simply didn't relish the thought of having the man about the place causing more disconcerting problems between them.

"Perhaps this would be an ideal time for me to take a break as he intends to devote quite a lot of his time to the children. My mother has been off colour lately and I really ought to go home", said Jill.

"If I were you, I'd take your break later when Sir Malcolm and Lady Sylvia come home, it would be a shame not to spend some time with Barry, especially as you and he are friends. I believe you are here on his recommendation!".

"Yes, but we met only briefly during his vacation in Devon", said Jill. She would have liked to confide in Michelle about the type of bastard he really was, but thought it best to keep it buried in the past where it belonged. Ah well, the problems were surmountable, after all she hated the ground he walked upon now, just about.

Jill lay in bed listening to the faint sound of classical cassette music coming from the adjacent bedroom occupied by Barry. Why did he have to come back into her life to torment her? Just a little longer and she would have been rid of the ghost for all time.

As she stared into the shadows her mind went back to the time she met him. A hush of recognition had fallen over the music room as he entered. Not being overly musical, Jill didn't immediately recognise him. It came to her gradually, although she couldn't put a name on him. She remembered admiring his physique, poised with his head held high, as he spoke to a group of young musicians who were practising. He was tall, well built with brown hair streaked with silver and wearing a beige linen suit; he had one of those long slim bodies on whom clothes looked stylish. His sun-tanned, sombre looking face became handsome as he smiled at a young girl violinist who in turn flushed and her eyes lit up at his words. Although the skin around his eyes showed lines, he looked younger than his photographs, his jawline sharp. She knew he was in his late thirties and had in the past a few ex-mistresses but had remained unmarried; he must have some flaws hidden underneath his showy exterior otherwise he would have been snapped up.

A boy pointed in Jill's direction and in a few long strides he was beside her.

"So you are the five year old's teacher?", he enquired with his head held slightly to one side.

"Yes! Yes I am! Can I be of any assistance to you?"

"May I have a loan of a group of, say.. three boys and three girls, under your surveillance of course, while I try out an arrangement I am working on?", he asked.

This was the most unheard of proposition she ever had to deal with so she instantly said, "I'm sorry Mr ..., we don't hire out children".

He flushed beneath his tan as he said, "Ah! You will hire them to me - where can I find your Head Master?".

"It is a Head Mistress actually, she can be found in her office; second left down the corridor", said Jill, dismissing him by turning her back and speaking to the children. "Right children, time to go back to the classroom".

She remembered the little ones obediently marching off, she followed them without a further glance at the handsome celebrity.

Next morning, Mrs Campbell, the Head Mistress came into her classroom excitedly saying, "You would never guess, Jill, Dr Barry Thorpe, the famous composer, wants you to take some children to the cottage he has taken for a month to try out a collection of tunes he is working on. Isn't it simply thrilling?".

She asked Jill to sort out the children most suitable and rushed off to arrange the mini bus to get them there by 11.00am.

It was obvious this damned man was used to getting

exactly what he demanded; his personal magnetism achieved everything for him. Jill was irritable as she chose carefully the children most likely to sing well together with the capacity for exhibiting their capabilities to the best advantage. It went against her grain to assist a man so cock sure of himself and who could attract every eye so dramatically.

As it happened the address on the card was just down the road from her parent's house - she knew it well. They never got to know the people staying there as they changed each month.

He met them at the door and ignored Jill, saying, "Good morning children, I hope you are all in good voice this fine morning".

The children chorused, "Yes, Dr Thorpe".

He put them into seats he had already set out for them and his love of children soon became apparent to her. He couldn't resist picking up an adorable little blond girl and setting her on his knee asked, "What is your name?".

"I'm Jessie", she whispered.

"I am going to teach you a song, but before I do, what would you like us all to sing?"

With her little finger stuck inside her mouth pushing out her cheek, she whispered, "Old MacDonald had a duck".

He threw back his head and laughed and Jill couldn't keep

her face straight either as their smiling eyes met above the little girl's head.

"What's your teacher's name?", he asked coyly, his chin pressing on her little blond head, his gaze still holding Jill's.

"Miss Ashton", she answered as she looked at Jill shyly.

That was it; she was putty in his hands from then on.

Two mornings a week she brought the children to the cottage for singing lessons.

From the first moment he touched her she was completely lost. It was on the second morning that she had taken the children to his holiday cottage. He asked them all to join hands and dance around in a circle. Joining in with the circle of children he held out his hand to her. As he clasped her hand firmly, she was in no doubt that his strong clasp conveyed a message and she curled her fingers tightly around his in response. It was obvious he was experienced in the art of seduction but she was stripped of her normal defence and was drawn to him like a magnet.

Mother didn't like him from the start, she sensed an uneasy shiftiness about him - she should have listened to her - mother's have a way of knowing things. Yes, she was right, it was a form of madness. Father liked him though, but then he was biased, he loved music.

It had been for the sake of silence and seclusion that Barry had hired the cottage in Devon so that he could fully occupy himself with composing. In today's world of traffic, crowds and telephones, solitude was a luxury, he had said.

She was to find out that he was able to generate massive interest, probable due to his aura of mystique, among the whole community and draw people and gain confidence.

He was endowed with a creative genius; she watched as he started the first fragments of a melody using just a few notes on the piano and became enchanted as it gradually turned into a full scale theme. Those little five year old children eventually went on the stage in school accompanied by the senior music students; they sang and danced like little angels while acting out their parts. The photographers from the local press came and a photograph was splashed all over the front page of Barry conducting the young musicians while the tots sang.

The written commentary below the picture read:
We were privileged by having in our community, Dr Barry Thorpe, who is unique in being a celebrated composer and also a genius on the piano. He thanked the Head Mistress, Mrs Campbell, of the Bebe School, Salcombe, for assisting him in composing a manual for educational purposes and music for instrumental beginners. The children who performed his work did him proud and he is hopeful that his visit will be an inspiration to them and that they will continue with their pursuit in music.

On the last evening before he was to leave, Jill and he were both despondent; with retrogression in the air he played the piano in a soft tone with a romantic expression before settling on the settee with their arms around each other.

"I am not looking forward to being separated from you, I can't bear the thought of it", Barry had said.

Jill shivered as they watched the smouldering, dying embers of the fire. "We don't have to be separated, I could get a teaching job anywhere. I'm sure they are two a penny in London. I'll go there!".

"No, my darling, I couldn't let you do that. When I get back to London I will be very, very busy and I wouldn't have anything like the time to devote to you that we have enjoyed here".

"Even a famous composer must have free time, you can't work twenty four hours a day or you wouldn't be worth tuppence. Please let me go, Barry!", she pleaded.

"I can't stop you and I would love to have you there, but I must pre-warn you, it will be different".

They both relaxed into each other's arms when she made the final decision of moving to London. The terrible ache of parting was lifted and they clung to each other in a passionate embrace until it was time for him to walk her home.

Mother was still up when she got in and when Jill informed her of her intention she nearly had a fit.

"I don't like this one bit, I think you are going to be badly hurt. You've only known him a month and it's well known that these famous people are only after one thing and they know there are always gullible people like you to give it to them".

"Mother you are wrong about Barry, he is one of the most decent people I have ever met and he has never once asked me to go to bed with him even though he probably wanted to, he has too much respect for me. I'm sure he loves me!".

"Oh Jill! Jill! Your naivety amazes me at times! I thought I could credit you with more common sense than to go running after a man who will think nothing of casting you aside at the drop of a hat, once he has had his way with you. Your attitude at the moment, while you are obsessed with this man, is similar to those poor devils in the asylum who have a distorted view of the world".

Yes, mother thought she was completely off her rocker and she simply didn't like him. She was right about the obsession Jill had for him - the very sight of the man could send her heart racing and enhance her moods.

Unfortunately she got the same reaction from Mrs Campbell when she handed in her notice.

"I trust you have thought long and hard before coming to this drastic decision, Jill; I would hate to see you hurt. I have been very proud of your record in this school and you have surpassed all the expectations I had for you. Unfortunately, once I accept your resignation I can't have you back if things don't work out. It is an irrevocable decision you will have made as I am honour bound to make a new appointment from the long waiting list of teachers wishing to work here".

"I won't want to come back, thank you, Mrs Campbell. I am certain I am doing the right thing and I'm sure it won't be too long before I get a teaching position in London".

She moved in with her friend, Maria, but it soon became apparent that teaching positions were few and far between in London. She could just about afford to keep herself for a few months, after that she would have to look for other types of employment. Barry was constantly rushing around with a crazy schedule and never had a spare moment with one thing or another. He was writing for music festivals and producing sound tracks for films and TV series. At that time he was also offering a course in composition at the Royal Academy and regularly adjudicating at competitions.

When they did find time to meet up, it was different; they didn't laugh together as much as they used to and she knew that Maria was worried about how little effort he made to see her as she always seemed to be the instigator of the meetings, more often than not hanging around to see him for short periods of time between his appointments.

The last occasion they met was on a night he had been feeling really low when she phoned. When she asked him why he was feeling so depressed, he answered, "In my profession we are prone to these lows, through over work".

"I'll take a taxi round to your flat and maybe I can cheer you up".

"I wouldn't if I were you, you'll only end up getting depressed as well", he had said urgently.

She went anyway and he looked terrible. The physique that had attracted her to him in the first instant was stooped. He went to his desk and sat down, his face ashen and lowered his head into his hands.

"My darling, please talk to me about whatever is troubling you - it might help", she had moved to his side and laid her hand gently on the back of his head.

He immediately flung her off with one rough movement, pushed back his chair and rose to his feet, sauntered over to the window and looked into the dark abyss beyond.

"You shouldn't have come here this evening. Why did you ignore my warning? I think you had better call a taxi as I have to catch an early plane in the morning".

The cruel reaction to her tenderness and words hurt her so much, it was the first time it had dawned on her that there was none so blind as those that wouldn't see. She started to shake as she pulled on her coat and went to the phone to commence dialling. He watched her for a while, probably feeling sorry for her, then suddenly in a few strides he was beside her and covered the hand that held the phone, pressed it down on the rest. He said to her, "I am sorry, Jill, please forgive me. I have good reason for my behaviour tonight and if I could change things for us, I would, but I can't".

She didn't understand or query his words but turned round and looked at him with tears starting to brim in her eyes. She simply said, "If I could change the way I feel about you, I would also; you see, I can't help loving you, Barry".

He drew her into his arms murmuring softly, "Oh Jill! Jill! It was never my intention for that to happen. My God, what have I done to you?". He kissed her tenderly at first then his lips became more demanding and urgent as they sought the inside of her mouth with his tongue and with a hunger she had never known him to possess previously. "My god, you are incredibly lovely and enticing", he murmured lecherously against her lips. Then he ran his hands sensually down over both her breasts, underneath her coat; disengaging her blouse he lowered his mouth to run his lips over her nipples, one after the other. Suddenly the gentleness changed to a lustful passion and his breathing became fast and shallow. In his rough treatment her coat was hoisted off her shoulders until it fell onto the floor. She could feel him against her, his sexual need obvious, as he asked hoarsely, "Do you want to stay with me tonight?".

It was a question that didn't need any pondering as she had never before experienced an actual physical pain deep within her body in the need to be close to someone as she had that night. As she gazed at him ecstatically, the question had only one answer, simply, "Yes".

Without any further ado and leaving her coat in a heap on the floor where it fell, he steered her towards the bedroom and hastily proceeded to undress her.

Likewise she reached out her hands to undress him. His melancholy disappeared as if by magic and they both laughed when zips stuck and again when he was left with nothing on but a shirt because she couldn't get the hang of the cufflinks. She became hot and bothered as his arousal disturbed and distracted her and in the end impatiently screamed, "Help!".

His hands were magic; the hands that thrilled the world were now thrilling her from top to toe as he delivered a breathless *forte*. He then started with his mouth, almost devouring her as he sensually lingered on her breasts before moving down her body, driving her crazy with desire.

She had made love to him in her mind many times but was completely astonished and unprepared for the emotions and sensations that were aroused within her as together they reached the heights of euphoria; she wanted to die in his arms, never let ordinary things touch her again.

During the night the slightest stir made by one set the other off and they seemed to spend most of the night making love.

When she awoke in the morning he was gone - he had left a note which simply said *'Jill. I told you I had to catch an early plane and as you were sound asleep, I didn't disturb you. Drop the key back through the letter box when you have locked the door. Barry'.*

She very badly needed a cuddle that morning, wouldn't
have minded if he had wakened her; she wanted to lie
lazily in his arms and be held close in the aftermath of
their night of love. It should have been an essential
commodity to conclude their night together, consequently
she felt maltreated and let down. These were the ordinary
things she didn't want touching her again - while she
should have felt happy, she felt sad and deflated, akin to
the aftermath of bingeing the night away on sweet German
wine and Belgian chocolates; oh so nice at the time but
disastrous for her figure.

It was 10.00am and she was in the shower, but wasn't
singing, when Maria rang from the bank. She had never
heard her so angry, "If you want to throw yourself at that
damned man, do so, but for God's sake let me know in
future if you're not coming home. I have been out of my
mind with worry since discovering you weren't there. Get
yourself home and wait there for me to call, I am going to
recommend you for a post going here at the bank".

How she got the job she'll never know as she looked like
death at the interview with so little sleep. She took
Maria's advice not to ring Barry again but to wait for him
to ring her. The following weeks were very painful as she
waited and waited in vain and it was about as much as she
could bear not to ring him. Indeed she did start to call his
number on occasions but the humiliation of a verbal
rejection saved her from dialling that last digit. Why had
she expected his love? She was nothing but a small town

girl, undistinguished and obscure who shirked the limelight and completely deficient in the practical musical know-how; there were endless numbers of exotic woman with self-assurance, charm and culture who were knowledgeable in music around every day available to him and he was indeed a rare breed; an eligible bachelor. He was also a bastard of the worst kind. Although they had made terrific love, part of him must have been detached and desensitised. The sheer bloody hypocrisy of it all hit her violently; it was completely beyond her comprehension how any man could have used a woman so despicably.

It had taken a long time to snuff out the flame and to get over the emotional damage he had inflicted on her, but with God's help she had emerged from it, practically, not giving a damn for the man.

For the first time since arriving in Ireland, Jill wished she was back home with her mother and father in South Hams, being lulled to sleep by the waves. At long last she succumbed and overslept in the morning.

Barry was sitting in her chair when she rushed into the class. Her cheeks were flushed and hair tousled, she almost retreated when she saw him but there was no hiding place.

"Good morning, children! Sorry I'm late ", to which they chorused, "Good morning, Jill".

"Thank you for seeing to the children, I simply couldn't

get to sleep last night", she admitted to Barry unable to conjure up an excuse.

"I didn't have a great night either; a certain disagreeable woman kept me awake, but when I don't sleep, for one reason or another, I still manage to get up in the morning".

She took it he boorishly referred to the night they spent together and was mortified and disgusted with him. The children were preoccupied with puzzles that he had given them to solve, so under her breath and for his ears only, she said, "They really broke the mould when they made you. I know you don't give a damn about me but does your type give a damn about anybody?".

"Yes, I care about these children!", he said quietly, as he glared at her.

"Well, although we are in stark contrast, we have at least one common purpose".

He raised himself out of her seat and stood back against the wall while she squeezed between him and the desk to reach her seat, her hips pressed against his firm body and she was conscious of his intake of breath. She sat down unperturbed and spoke to the children, "We will have our usual prayer. All together now!".

Clasping hands under their chins they closed their eyes and rhymed together - "Please God, send your angels to watch over us and keep us from sin. Do not lead us into temptation and deliver us from the evil one. Amen".

Barry looked back as he reached the door and over the children's heads met Jill's accusing gaze.

As he walked towards the music room he tried to interpret what was going through her mind and felt a deep sadness. She now looked upon him as 'the evil one' who had led her into temptation and sin.

As his fingers softly played a melancholy tune he thought back to the first time he set eyes on her and a few days later when he decided to seduce her. She wasn't his type at all, lacked the sophistication of the woman in the musical extravaganza world he belonged to, but was eye-catching. Her big blue eyes, fair skin and hair attracted him. She was long legged with full rounded breasts and hips. He had wanted her from the moment his eyes met hers over the little girl's head. The sun caught her eyes as she smiled at him, becoming a gorgeous light shade and as they twinkled they seemed to speak a language of their own.

It was on their next meeting that she responded to his seduction tactics and his heart sang. He hadn't banked on the sheer innocence of the girl and the sexual frolic he had in mind for his stay in Salcombe, never màterialised.

She had all the qualities sophisticated, sexy women lacked; she possessed an air of fragility and vulnerability that made him want to protect her, even from himself. She was such fun to be with and he had never enjoyed a time in his life more.

The beautiful area basked in a peculiarly clement climate

and they walked hand in hand through the palm, orange and lemon trees that fringed the bay; lay half asleep in the sun in the daisy strewn grass above the beach, sharing with the larks their exultant liberation; watched contently together as the surfers, water-skiers and boatmen ruled the waves while horses cantered over the white sands. She invigorated him with the joys of life, picnicing on the rocks at Starehole Bay and playing on the sands enjoying the bays and nooks.

At every opportunity he made excuses to be with her. When he wasn't working on composing the educational manual, he dreamt up reasons to visit her school in the hope of just another glimpse of her.

Late in the evening it became cool and he would never forget the cosiness they shared sitting together by the fire, wrapped up in each other's arms, in the cottage. Fulfilment for both of them was simply to touch, kiss, hold each other close, disclose the many funny revelations of the day that working with children presented and kiss again. She loved to hear him play well known, favourite and adored pieces on the well tuned piano - he played for her with a fresh mind as if he had just come upon new and fascinating discoveries. On occasions, he sang country songs to her with the aid of a guitar he unearthed from the top of a wardrobe.

She was a soft desirable woman and once on such an evening, while holding her gaze he watched her pupils dilate as he unbuttoned her blouse to expose her bra-less rounded breasts; he bent down to kiss each breast and enlarged pointed nipples. Although flustered she cradled his head against her supple, warm and smooth softness until he decided enough was enough and dutifully did up her buttons, then drew her into his arms again and held her tenderly against him.

As he played the pianissimo now, thoughts stirred the blood and he gradually replaced the melancholy tune with a louder beat until he was thumping the piano at a deafening pitch, eventually coming to a crescendo by crashed both hands heavily on the keys.

Laying his head in his hands across the piano keys he shuddered as he recalled his handling of the predicament that had evolved. He should never have continued the affair beyond Devon. It had been a beautiful, tender and romantic time in his life, she had made him feel young again. He should have been able to look back on that time with cherished memories, instead, all he could think of now, was that it had been the premature ruination of a sweet, innocent girl.

He had no such time to devote to her in London and although as enchanting as ever she did not fit into his lifestyle any more.

What possessed him to let her come to the flat that evening while he had been in such a depressed and shattered state? That very day Sir Malcolm had rang him with the terrible news that the two badly charred bodies were coming home for burial. He couldn't get a flight till the morning and was in no state to entertain or indeed be entertained; nor had he any intention of talking about his two beloved friends to her.

She must intuitively have known their relationship was on the way out; the last thing he needed was serious involvement with another woman. They had been good for each other in Devon and he had been proud at his strength of character in never abusing her purity.

No! He should never have let her come to him, it would have been better all round for everyone. His breathing became difficult as he remembered with excitement, taking her succulent, overripe body that night; the endearments fell easily from her lips as their smooth love making rhythm gathered momentum and they were completely taken over by their need of each other.

In the morning, as he knotted his tie, he looked down at her sleeping form, she had a fulfilled and contented expression on her beautiful glowing face. She looked as innocent as the day she was born - one could become addicted to her body - even love her. As he dragged on the jacket of his suit he had shivered at the thought and turned quickly away, knowing she would be better off without someone like him. No woman would ever be able to cope with his deranged complexities.

Her demands on him the night previous to the funeral had left him absolutely shattered and it showed through in his ashen face and black rings around his eyes. Sir Malcolm put his hand on his back and said, "Christ, Barry, you are taking this worse than any of us". It was, however, one of the saddest occasions in his life, he had been devastated by it all and his life had taken on a new meaning as he looked on the four desolate children.

In the days following he had made up his mind that when he got back to London, on the next occasion that Jill rang him, he would tell her to forget him. As it happened, she never rang, therefore, in a way he didn't actually have to hurt her with words, but she would have been devastated anyway. Little did she know that she would be well rid of him. When her body squeezed past his this morning, he felt the desire intensify within him, but knew that, although he wanted to, he should never have the privilege of laying a finger on her again.

Chapter Four

They were placing the last basket into the Space Waggon when Jane called that Michelle was wanted on the telephone.

"I'm afraid there has been an accident", Jane said to Jill when Michelle was out of earshot, "Patrick is in hospital".

Jill and Jane waited anxiously for Michelle to come back while the children played happily around the car oblivious to the fact that the trip could be off.

Barry had his arm around Michelle's shoulder when they emerged.

"I am taking Michelle to the hospital", he said, "A crate of wine has fallen on Patrick's head and he is in hospital, unconscious".

"Oh, Michelle, please try not to worry", said Jane, "The chances are he will be alright".

Michelle, in shock and obviously trying to psyche herself up for the visit to the hospital, said, "We can't deprive the children, they have thought of nothing else for days. Perhaps Jack would run me to the hospital, then if Barry didn't mind, he could take my place on the outing".

Jack had heard the fuss from where he had been weeding the flower bed and made his way hurriedly towards them hollering, "What's all the hullabaloo? Anything I can do?".

Everything was under control in no time and they all shrieked their good wishes after Michelle as they drove off in haste, Jack behind the wheel.

Jill looked at Barry and said hopefully, "Take no notice of what Michelle said, I'm quite capable of taking the children on my own; I'm sure you are busy".

"Doing what? I came here to be with the children and I have seen precious little of them. I would love to come today, that is if the children want me".

The children all made it quite clear that they were in favour of Barry coming along.

"Uncle Barry, can we take Milly? She comed with us swimming one day, and nobody", she moved her head from side to side as she spoke, "knew she was there?", said Bonny dramatically.

She stood expectantly, with big wide appealing eyes, awaiting Barry's reply while she almost choked the cat.

Jane came to the cat's rescue by disengaging it from Bonny's tight grip, saying, "I'm sorry, Milly has to catch the little mouse that's been hiding in the cupboard for days".

Barry's eyes met Jill's and smiled over Bonny's head as he whipped the child off her feet and swung her up onto the high seat and clasped her in.

Jill knew for certain as she smiled back that history hadn't a snowflake's chance in hell of repeating itself where she and Barry were concerned. The nerve of the man! If he wanted another fling he had better think again.

He disappeared into the house and came back wearing khaki coloured shorts and sporting a colourful red flat cap more suited to the golf course. He settled into the driving seat and as they drove off he winked at her then led the children into song, 'Old MacDonald had a farm'. They absolutely loved him, he had the knack of making the commonplace seem remarkable.

"Uncle Barry", Jamie yelled when the song came to an end, "Jill knit me a new jumper and she is going to knit the other's one as well".

"Ah, sure by gorra isn't it just great", said Barry, imitating Jack's accent, to the children's delight.

Leaving Skibbereen behind they drove along the coast road. The verges were speckled with sheep treading carefully along crevices of rock. They came to Crookhaven, a delightful little village on the crook of Cork's south westerly peninsula with a terrific view of yachts coming and going.

Barry asked directions from Iain how to get to Barley Cove, the beautiful sandy beach with its lovely sweep of golden sands, that they had all been to on a previous occasion. Jill advised against bathing as the water temperature was a little on the cool side. "Take no notice of her, sure she's a woman and they're soft, in more ways than one".

Barry and the children threw off their clothes and ran straight into the sea while Jill laughed at their antics. When they were all dried and dressed he and the boys played a game of cricket while Jill and Bonny made sand castles.

The faint voice of Iain, almost blocked out by the sound of the waves, reached Jill's ears, "Uncle Barry, last time you played cricket with us, daddy beat you".

Barry's voice came back shakily, "Yes, you're right, so he did".

When they were all bowled out, Barry and Jill packed the children into the car again amid Jamie's excited chatter at having scored the most runs.

They drove on as far as Mizen Head with its striking vast vertical cliffs which, though spectacular, looked frightening and dangerous for children.

They stopped to picnic at Bantry House with its spectacular views overlooking Bantry Bay. Jill and Barry were enchanted by the magnificent scene. "The view from here has been proclaimed as disputably one of the finest in the world", said Barry.

Later on in the day, when at Glengarriff, Barry surprised the boys by producing a fishing rod. They squealed boisterously in excitement.

"Ah! Best kept secret of the day! You didn't know that I brought it, did you? I sneaked it in when you were all in the car. I assure you we shall have baked fillets of brill for supper".

He handed the rod to Jill while he fastened string to a stick. He then tied on a foul piece of cheese that he had rescued from the bin and handed it to Bonny so that she would not be outdone.

Jumping up and down and in her excitement shrieked, "Bloody hell!", which brought howls of laughter from the boys.

"What?", said Barry in controlled annoyance.

Jill's eyes, as they met his above Bonny's head, begged him not to reprimand her further. This needed diplomacy and time to sort out the best way to deal with it. They both let loose suppressed smiles and Bonny went off happily dabbling the line in the water, raising it often to see if she had caught a fish.

Each boy in turn had a lesson on how to attach the bait to the hook and throw the line. At long last Alan hooked what they all thought must be a real beauty. Alas, the catch, when landed, consisted of a tiny little sea trout which Barry decided to throw back to live and fight another day.

When it was Barry's turn, a large trout was lured by a bread flake and took. He shouted excitedly, "This is more like it".

He played the big five pounder for a full twenty minutes,

but to everyone's dismay, it got away.

The weather suddenly deteriorated and they all packed into the car. The rain came tumbling down and there was less chance of seeing more of the fascinating seascapes. They could just about make out the hazy forms of sheep trotting some way ahead, in the soft mist. They continued round twisting roads amid the sheen of heather, past isolated farmhouses and between the massive rock formations that broke the skyline and were the backbone of the mountains.

The weather in this part of Ireland may not be predictable but the welcoming charm of the Irish was always warm and could be relied on, so they eventually made their way back to Glengarriff and took solace in the Eccles Hotel, set on the shores of the harbour overlooking Bantry Bay.

Corkonians are widely regarded as the most talkative of all the Irish and Dominic Murphy, the hotel proprietor, was no exception. He extended an unsurpassed friendly welcome by captivating the children with his chatter and relating to Barry and Jill the delights of Bantry Bay, as they warmed around a cosy open fire.

Jill ordered a hot Irish coffee with whisky, topped with cream while Barry simply had tea. "I'm a born again tea drinker, I think it was the chimp advert that did it", he said to the happy laughter of the children.

The children each guzzled down a massive sundae of layered ice cream, jelly and fruit. They were utterly exhausted and all fell asleep in the car on the drive home.

The tension between Barry and Jill, which had temporarily lifted during the day, came back with a vengeance as the strains surfaced until the atmosphere could be cut with a knife.

How he had the audacity to come back into her life when he knew she must hate him for what he had done to her, was simply beyond comprehension.

"I still can't understand why you came here and I would like you to tell me why you recommended me for this job?", she asked.

"I knew you were a damn good teacher and that you were available".

She checked on the children before saying, "Are you sure it wasn't because I was easy and a damn good lay and there just might be another chance".

He didn't answer straight away but she could see he was seething. His knuckles turned white as he gripped the steering wheel. "That is offensively ridiculous and you know it? If that had been my objective, I need not have dragged you here. I don't particularly care much for your choice of words either; a woman reaching twenty four and still a virgin couldn't exactly be described as easy".

Why had she said such a stupid thing? He was right of course, he could have had her any day or night while in London, not even for the asking, just for the taking, but he plainly didn't want her.

"I was easy and you know it".

"Anyone who is in love is easy".

"I suppose it was rather obvious that I loved you just as I hope it is obvious now how much I detest you. It must be nice to know you have robbed a woman you do not love of her virginity. Do men boast about how many virgins they have deflowered? Or do they just gloat inwardly to themselves?".

"I can only answer for one man and he certainly didn't boast, nor did he gloat. To answer the question of why I came to Checkerberry, I would like you to know that I have a very legitimate reason for visiting". Then, after a brief pause, he added, "Teresa and Geoff would have wanted me to guide and oversee their children".

"Isn't that the responsibility Sir Malcolm and Lady Sylvia have acquired?".

He answered the question guardedly, biding his time, "They are old-timers with lots of experience behind them but know little on how to bring up modern children".

It was indisputable, this man who could treat women like smut, was willing, if need be, to take on the full responsibility of his friend's children.

"Barry! Laying my feelings aside, I would like to thank you for making today such a memorable day for the children".

Her words surprised him and he took his eyes off the road for a second to glance at her. "No need to thank me, you two young ladies would have been just as capable, perhaps even more so. I have noticed the pleasure you both get from pleasing the children"

"No, the children enjoyed today because you were there. They probably would have enjoyed themselves with us, but it wouldn't have been memorable ".

"Do you know what I admire about you?".

"No",

"You give credit where it is due, regardless of the grudge you hold" .

"I wish I didn't ever have to hold a grudge against anyone, it's not in my nature", she said with her head lowered.

Alan stirred , "Are we near home yet?".

"Not long now", replied Jill, leaning over and tucked the rug around him.

"I need to clear the air about something, Jill, I don't think it is appropriate to speak of it now but will you come to the music room after dinner?".

"Very well".

The children were over excited when they got back. Barry carried Bonny straight to bed as she was in a sound sleep. While giving the boys their supper Jane had to endure a long blow-by-blow account of the day, and the inevitable memory that would stay with them for ever, of the one that got away.

Michelle hadn't returned but she rang to report that Patrick had recovered consciousness. He had a whale of a headache but was already joking about his mishap and charming the pants off the nurses.

Barry stopped playing the piano as Jill entered the music room, which he regarded as his sanctuary. "Are they all asleep?", he asked as he rose from the stool.

"Oh, I wouldn't say that, but tucked in. They are talking about the next time already. It is heart breaking and such a terrible shame that they have lost their parents, they obviously miss out on occasions like today", she said with a sigh.

Barry's expression emphasised his deep rooted pain as he spoke. "God forbid that they should ever miss out on anything". He suddenly took a step towards her and looked her straight in the eye as he spoke.

"Jill, I am not going to apologise for what happened between us, because I think you knew the score. If you hadn't agreed, it would never have happened. I may be a bastard in your eyes, but regardless of how immoral you judge me, you will have to agree that I am not a rapist. What I want to know is, are we both mature enough to put it behind us and go from here on a different footing, after all I am not going to disappear into thin air, I intend visiting the children at every opportunity I can get".

Give the devil his due; he had warned her of the consequences should she move to London. The onus had been on herself that night to stay, also, would any other way of letting her down have been less hurtful?

"You won't ever lay a finger on me again?".

"I won't ever lay a finger on you again".

"This time it will be purely platonic?".

"Purely platonic".

"Very well! For the sake of the children - Done!", she said as she extended her hand.

He took her hand in a tight grip enticingly and when the urge to curl her fingers around his in response was strong she pulled with such strength that she almost toppled over.

"Good!", he said as he took a step backwards, "I would like to see each of the children to find out how much they have learnt from Joseph".

Dare she tell him that they had learnt more from Patrick about how the San Diego Chargers faced the New York Giants across the line of scrimmage and how the quarter back missed the signal and had to start again before he called the team into a huddle behind the ...

"Well, Joseph has been on holiday for quite a while but asked me to try and encourage them to practice while he was away".

"Did you have any success?".

"I am afraid Alan and Iain aren't that musically inclined but they practised a bit under duress". She hesitated before continuing, "I'll let you find out about Jamie for yourself. Bonny of course has a good singing voice for her age but hasn't started any instruments".

Barry smiled, "I'll see Bonny first, simply for fun; we can't have her feeling left out".

He walked to the highly polished Steinway grand piano and without sitting down stretched down his hands and strummed a melody with long graceful fingers.

"This piano was mine! I promised Teresa I would let her have it, but unfortunately, before I got it shipped over, sh.. she died. Music was a dominant theme in her life as it was in her maternal grandfather before her. She possessed an old battered piano and was an accomplished player. Apparently music is a thing that runs in families so Geoff and she hoped the children would be musical". His voice was uneven and trembled slightly. It was obvious they were very close, her death must have been a severe blow to him.

He turned round abruptly, "Would tomorrow mid-morning suit for me to have Bonny?".

"Yes", replied Jill, "Mid-morning would suit very nicely".

She closed the door quietly and the faint delicate strains of Beethoven's 'Moonlight Sonata' accompanied her as she made her way, along the corridor to join Jane.

When she entered the sitting room Jane remarked, "We are so privileged to have such a musical genius in our midst. In the evening, he plays softly; while the children are playing, he plays happily; occasionally, he plays mournfully and those of us that loved them as he did, appreciate that".

Tears welled up in Jane's eyes as she searched for her handkerchief.

Barry sat Bonny up on a stool beside the piano, "What would you like me to play for you?".

She put her little head back, pursed her lips as she looked at the ceiling deep in thought then announced, "Jingle bells".

"But it's not Christmas! Think again".

She went through the same procedure, this time with her eyes closed tight, then jumped up and down excitedly, "Jesus loves me".

Barry smiled happily, then he thought of something. "Bonny, bloody hell is one of the naughty things people aren't supposed to say. Jesus wouldn't like to hear you say naughty words. Where did you hear it?". It was the sort of thing anybody could say; himself perhaps.

"Mummy said it", said Bonny unperturbed.

Barry couldn't believe his ears; her mother was dead such a long time. Bonny would only have been three.

"When did mummy say it?".

"One day when you were there and daddy was cross with her".

"Where were you, Bonny?", he asked anxiously.

"Just there; then I runned away", she answered becoming bored or perhaps everything else was blocked out except for the row.

"Bonny, mummy was upset when she said the naughty words, she wouldn't want you to say them".

"I won't ever say the naughty words again, Uncle Barry. Are you going to play Jesus Loves Me now?".

"Right this minute! You'll have to sing though, so that my fingers can find the right notes".

He had been unnerved by her words and was saddened that her memory, perhaps the only memory of her mother, was a bad one. He looked at her now with pride as she sang, shaping her mouth with each word. She will definitely be a singer, he thought. A soprano.

Later in the afternoon Jamie ventured in. Barry looked at him pitifully. He was a quiet little boy, didn't show his feelings much. He must miss Geoff, he had undoubtedly been Geoff's favourite.

"Well, Jamie, so how is the piano practising coming along?".

Jamie lowered his head, "Jill said it was alright for me not to practice because my fingers weren't long enough".

"Ah! Did she now? I think they are, you know, so lets have a little try".

Jamie slouched over the piano awkwardly and with difficulty tried to extend his hand over the white keys.

Barry stopped him immediately.. "You'll never play with that bad posture. Sit up straight, in a nice relaxed position. That's better", he said as Jamie made an effort to straighten. "Spread out your fingers over the keys and just warm your muscles, taking it nice and steady".

After fifteen minutes Barry said, "You're going to need a lot of practice as you keep forgetting where to put your fingers for the scale".

Jamie's gaze went to the top shelf, then he said, "I know where to put my fingers on the flute".

Looking surprised, Barry followed his gaze then went

over and reached up for the highly polished unfamiliar flute. It gleamed as he turned it over and examined it, then handed it to Jamie without a word.

Jamie took the flute and stood up, then caressed it lovingly before pressing it to his lips, he laid his fingers on the keys with perfect precision. He looked straight ahead and swayed his body ever so slightly to the tune.

The music that reached Barry's ears had a warm golden tone. He was overcome with emotion as he sat down and softly accompanied Jamie on the piano to the tune of 'Down by the Sally Gardens', the musical interpretation by Charles V. Stamford of W B Yates's poem.

At the end of the tune Jamie took the flute from his lips and grinned from ear to ear proudly.

"So Joseph taught you to play the flute?", said Barry smiling.

"No", said Jamie, "Jill taught me".

"Is that so?", said Barry taken by surprise.

"Yes! It's Jill's flute! She tried us all with it but I was the only one that took to it, so she taught me three tunes".

"You're good Jamie! Really good!", he said with emotion. "I'm so proud of you, and Jill for discovering your talent. It will be hard work you know, nothing comes easy. Are you ready for it?".

66

"yeah!" can I
get proper lessons?".

"Yeah", said Barry with a grin.

Jamie, in his excitement, knocked over a chair and didn't stop to pick it up.   He ran calling, "Jill, Jill, guess what.....".

Five minutes later Jill appeared round the door. From the far end of the room he watched as she approached, her blond hair hung casually on her shoulders, her light blue eyes alive and twinkling. She never failed to stun him with her striking good looks. He glanced at the pendant around her throat that lay loosely between her breasts on a gold chain. His glance brought a flush across her skin. He knew she was remembering the day he gave it to her. She hadn't wanted to accept it; it was the first decent piece of jewellery she ever had in her life.

Handing her the flute, he said, "Aren't you the dark horse! Why didn't you tell me last summer?".

"Oh, how could I? You being a musical genius".   She caressed the polished flute tenderly just as Jamie had done, "I've never played for anyone other than my father. He taught me".

"I have my limitations you know, I can't play the flute. At one time I played and experimented with the clarinet but I'm not good on wind instruments. I appreciate the splendid effect of them and what they can do to a Symphony", he said.

"Do you know anyone who could teach Jamie?".

"Yes, I know someone who is marvellous, right here in Cork. I'll arrange for him to listen to Jamie with a view to having him taught".

Chapter Five

One couldn't put a finger on when the transformation had occurred, but occur it did. Everything ran smoothly until the late Autumn. Jill's holiday was long overdue and if it hadn't been for her mother falling ill it would have remained so.

It was Alan and Iain's ninth birthday. Sir Malcolm, Lady Sylvia and Barry had flown in that morning as a surprise for the twins. The children and adults alike had thoroughly enjoyed the birthday celebrations and were pleasantly tired when the news came of Jill's mother's illness and that her father wanted her home.

When the children realized she was going away there was bedlam. All four of them clung to her in the bedroom as she packed. The initial teacher/pupil relationship had been well and truly transformed to mother/child familiarity.

To whom or what the blame could be apportioned was indefinable. What she knew for certain was that these children were very, very frightened. They had lost their mother and father, they now felt they were in grave danger of losing her.

She looked into the frightened faces of Alan and Iain, and although a lot was expected of them because they were the eldest, they were still very young and vulnerable. She held them close, a little head on each breast. It was this touching little scene that Sir Malcolm and Barry encountered as they walked into her bedroom.

"I want to go with Jill", sobbed Bonny holding fast to a pleat on Jill's skirt. Barry whisked her up and sat her stride legged on one hip while he drew Jamie to him with his free hand.

Sir Malcolm reaching over and patted Jamie's head saying, "Everything is going to be just fine, just fine". This all-powerful man, educated at Eton and Trinity College, Cambridge, knighted for deeds such as saving the bank from heavy losses and collapse against all the odds, was totally at sea in this domestic situation.

From the day it had been built the bedroom would never have held more people as Lady Sylvia, Jane and Michelle arrived *en masse*. "I've got an idea", said Lady Sylvia, "While Jill is away you can all have a little holiday in London with Grandpa and I. Won't that be exciting?".

"I don't want to go", said Alan, wiping a tear that was running down his cheek.

"Why? There are lots of exciting things to do and see in London".

Iain answered for both of them, saying, "Last time you kept us, Mummy and Daddy didn't come back".

"I won't be away for long, children, I promise you. As a matter of fact when you come back from Grandma and Grandpa's, more than likely I'll be here waiting for you", she said encouragingly.

Barry spoke for the first time. "Jill you have enough on your plate at the moment, we will get this all sorted out when you're gone. You've only fifteen minutes till we leave so that you can catch that plane".

Throwing him a worried glance while trying to hold back the tears, she pressed the last item of clothing into her travelling case and snapped it shut. Amid their anguish she kissed each child goodbye.

As she and Barry made their way to the airport, they both knew the problem was more complicated than how long she was going to be away.

"Perhaps, in a way I am to blame", said Jill, giving in to tears and sat dabbing her eyes.

"Perhaps!", replied Barry, "But then we're all to blame collectively, together with events".

Sir Malcolm and Lady Sylvia should maybe have come home more often and if Patrick hadn't had the accident, perhaps Michelle would have been more attentive. Jane shouldn't have given in to their whims and let them run to Jill with problems when she shouldn't have been disturbed at all while off duty. Barry had started coming more often lately and usually involved Jill in treats he had in mind for the children. Perhaps, most of all, Jill shouldn't have let them into her bed when they had a disturbed night.

They sat silently, buried in their own thoughts, each racking their brains as to what might be best for the children. The silence was broken when Barry asked a personal question, "Have you any involvements with anyone, Jill, men I mean?".

She thought that would have been crystal clear as she answered, "No, none whatsoever".

"You obviously intend getting married sometime in the future?".

"Well, I'm reasonably normal in thinking that is the expected eventuality but it wouldn't worry me one way or another if I didn't. I suppose I'd miss having children if I didn't".

"Would you ever consider marrying me, Jill?".

"I beg your pardon?". She heard, but the question seemed ludicrous.

"Will you marry me?".

"No". A lovely warm feeling encircled her. At last she could say no and really mean it.

"Why, for God's sake?".

His tone of voice conveyed his difficulty in grasping the fact that any woman, in her right mind, would turn him down.

"I don't love you! It's as simple as that and I'm not inclined to join the risk business. Also, I don't think it's the best idea you've ever had", she answered smugly.

"You don't have to love me! I know we have our differences, but then again, we have proved over the past months that we can be harmonious and we have one common dominator, we both love the children. I know you are tolerant and open to new experiences; look at the way you came to Ireland, you had no guarantees then".

"Ah, well, that was different, I needed to get away. Being a hermit was attractive to me".

"Why, Jill? Why did you want to be a hermit?".

She ignored the question saying, "If the children are the only reason you want to marry me, you needn't have bothered asking as we would never get them, we have no legal rights".

"We all have the children's best interest at heart and although Geoff and Teresa didn't name me as legal guardian, there is a clear understanding between Sir Malcolm, Lady Sylvia and myself. I've been around since they were born; I'm their Uncle Barry. I could adopt them, there will be no problems in that court at all".

Jill was about to go through to the departure lounge when Barry said, "I'm sorry Jill, this whole episode has taken over from your personal problems. Please give your mother and father my best wishes. Don't dismiss my proposition out of hand just yet, put it behind you for a few days then consider it again when you have your family sorted out".

He picked up her gloved hand and kissed it, "Goodbye, I

hope you find all well at home".

Jill was exhausted by the time she arrived at South Hams. Her father stood bare headed by the car with the most sombre look on his face she had ever seen. She ran straight into his arms saying, "It's not that bad father, is it?".

"Yes, I'm afraid it is, Jill. Your aunt Alice is with her now".

Aunt Alice and she embraced at the door as she entered, then she went straight through to her mother's bedroom.

Jill was shocked at how frail her mother had become in such a short time and she ran to her covering her face with kisses.

"Isn't this a caper! You coming home to watch me die", her mother smiled weakly.

She was a sharp and intelligent woman and knew her chances of survival were nil and accepted it with dignity.

"I wish I'd listened to you, Mother, I should never have left", said Jill sadly.

"That wouldn't have prolonged my life, my dear, you were right to go, but not in the circumstances you did".

Without saying I told you so, her voice may have been weaker and her eyes wearier but her message was as strong as ever, she said, "You have had a bad experience with that man and I know he has come back into your life but heed my words, to rekindle the infatuation you had for him would cause nothing but gloom and doom!". She closed her eyes and furrowing her forehead as she repeated the miserable words, "...gloom and doom!".

Jill quickly took her mother's hand in hers and spoke convincingly, "Mother, he can never hurt me again. One has to love to be hurt and I don't love him; the children are all I care about now".

Her mother relaxed back into the bed as she breathed, "Thank God! Thank God".

Within a few days she had sunk into unconsciousness and Jill, her father and Aunt Alice dismally witnessed her last breath.

It was a miserable day for the funeral, dark and cold enough for snow. The relations were in floods of tears, she had only just passed her fifty fifth birthday. "She was a good woman, your mother; blessed with the gift of second sight", one of the female relations whispered to Jill. She didn't cry at the funeral, she had done all her crying the few days previous to her death. She was only thankful that she hadn't hung on to suffer.

The most heart-breaking part of all for Jill was the sight of her father, at the station, being left alone to cope with his grief.

She felt numb as she said to him, "I'll come home soon father, this job of teaching the children privately can't last much longer. It was never meant to be permanent".

"My love, you have your life to lead, I'll be content with occasional visits and don't forget your Aunt Alice only lives down the road. The main thing now is your happiness - go out and seek it my girl".

She kissed him goodbye, having decided against telling him about Barry's proposal, although she knew nothing would have made him happier than his little girl marrying a famous composer, as music was probably his one passion left in life.

She turned thoughts of his marriage proposal over in her mind while in the plane and wondered if the proposal still stood; once he had time to give it more consideration he might decide never to broach the subject again; after all she had turned him down. Proposing to her had been the only way he could get the life he wanted, obviously a wife was mandatory for him to achieve his objective.

It was evident that Sir Malcolm and Lady Sylvia were unsuited to bringing up the children. Unwittingly the children had become attached to her and vice versa. Now that Barry had sown the seed in her mind, she felt she would do almost anything to get them. Yes, even marry a man she had fallen out of love with and who didn't love her.

Jill hardly recognised Barry as she came through the customs. The temperature was below normal for this time of year. With his heavy brown tweed coat and matching hat he was the most charismatic man in the arrivals lounge.

His first words were to convey his sympathy on the death of her mother and as she thanked him he gave her an encouraging pat on the shoulder.

Picking up the travelling bag he ignored the plump woman's words of recognition and adulation as she said to her friend. "Isn't that Barry Thorpe, the composer who is appearing tomorrow night at the Opera House? Isn't he handsome in the flesh?".

Suddenly there was a scurry as a young female reporter appeared from nowhere. "Dr Thorpe, could I have a few words with you please?". She proceeded to wave her identification in front of Barry's eyes which read 'The Cork Examiner'.

"I'm sorry, I really haven't time. I'm here to meet a friend".

"Will you be appearing tomorrow night, Dr Thorpe?", she persisted.

He became irritated at the stupid question. "My name is on the programme, isn't it? Barring accidents, I'll be there".

"Joanne Debussy's name is not on the programme. Did you know that she will also be appearing?".

"Please excuse me" Barry replied in a none too genteel fashion, as he guided Jill forcefully ahead of him.

As they drove off Barry said, "If you decide to marry me you'll have to get used to that sort of thing".

He drove to the expensively modern looking Jury's Hotel on the Western Road, situated amid beautiful gardens on the river-bank. "We need to talk, Jill, let's do it in pleasant surroundings".

As they stepped into the hotel foyer the manager came straight away to their rescue, when Barry was once again recognised by a group of people who asked for autographs, by guiding them past a magnificent ornamental waterfall into a separate lounge.

"Well", said Barry to Jill, with an impish grin, as the manager waited for their drinks order, "Am I going to order champagne or a whisky to drown my sorrows?".

Jill smiled coyly, then answered, "I've decided on champagne".

"I always knew you were a wise dame". He reached over and kissed her on the mouth in full view of the captivated manager, who straight away sussed out the situation and raised both his hands in delight. "The champagne is on the house! My congratulations, Dr Thorpe, to yourself and the good lady who has accepted your proposal in my presence".

When he came back with the champagne, he said to them,

"I will keep it a secret until you leave, but once your foot is over the door, I will broadcast it to everyone in the hotel".

"That couldn't be more fair", said Barry smiling gratefully.

They clicked glasses and drank to their future.

"Are you happy?", he asked attentively.

"Yes, I'm happy for us because we are going to acquire the children".

"Are you not the slightest bit happy that you are marrying a famous man?".

She shrugged nonchalantly, "No, it doesn't have any effect on me at all. Maybe I would even have preferred it if you weren't famous".

"Same goes for me, I would prefer not to be famous, but I love music".

Barry fumbled in his pocket, extracted a package and handed it to her. She drew out the most beautiful ring she had ever seen. It was an unusual cluster of dazzling marcasite and she loved it on sight.

He watched her reaction intently with pleasure. "Being famous and rich has it's advantages, so we shouldn't knock it. There will be plenty of diamonds in your life but I searched for something different for now. I will have it altered to fit your finger".

It fitted perfectly. Suddenly, woe betide! She felt cold as a mirage of her mother's dead face and her words 'Gloom and doom' dulled the sparkling and she shivered uncontrollably. Picking up the glass she held it to her lips but was unable to steady her trembling hand. He withdrew the glass and laid it on the gold tubular surrounded glass topped table as he shuffled to her side. He placed an encouraging arm around her shoulders, "Everything will be alright, you'll see!", he assured her.

The following morning Jill approached Sir Malcolm's office, almost as nervously as that first day when he had offered her the position. She knocked timidly and opened the door cautiously. "Far from being bogeymen - the currency dealers, whose only crime was to recognise that the pound was not worth what they pretended it to be - have done us all a good turn ... Oh Jill! Come and join us!", said Sir Malcolm gesturing copiously.

"Sorry, I'm interrupting, you two men have more important things to discuss. I'll come back later".

"If it's to do with my grandchildren, there's nothing more important as far as I'm concerned".

Barry stood up and spoke for the first time, "I asked Jill to join us. We have a matter of great delicacy to discuss with you, Sir Malcolm. I think it might be best if you rang for Lady Sylvia".

Sir Malcolm, a man of keen perception, asked no further

questions and rang through to the morning room asking Lady Sylvia to join them, "We are going to have a meeting", he concluded.

Presently Lady Sylvia arrived with her usual unpretentious grace, she smiled at everyone, sat down then gestured for Barry and Jill to take the seats at each side of her.

Barry said, "Thank you, Lady Sylvia, but I will take the seat next to Jill, if you don't mind".

She nodded her approval and moved over. Sir Malcolm cunningly observed the situation as he relaxed into his chair.

All eyes focused on Barry as he started to speak, "Jill and I have known each other for well over a year now and at long last she has consented to be my wife".

The announcement came as a shock as nobody suspected they had anything in common. Lady Sylvia was baffled, there had been no signs of a budding romance or otherwise between them. Jill was taken by surprise at his choice of words and refrained, by the skin of her teeth, from gasping.

Suddenly they were being congratulated and swamped by kisses, cuddles and handshakes.

"You crafty old devil", said Sir Malcolm as he proceeded to slap Barry heftily on the back.

Lady Sylvia said excitedly, "Don't you think the rest of the staff should be in on this. I suggest we celebrate properly with champagne in the drawing room".

With a commanding tone Barry said, "Please sit down", to which they obediently did.

"I did mention that we had a matter of delicacy to discuss. Well, the fact is we both love the children and wish to adopt them".

The worst possible situation Barry could imagine himself in was to have his proposal opposed and he wasn't prepared for Sir Malcolm's words. "Oh, now Barry, marrying the lovely Jill is one thing, but getting my grandchildren is another and I'm afraid there is no question of them ever being adopted by yourself or anyone else for that matter".

Lady Sylvia had gasped at Barry's proposal and was now expressing her full agreement with Sir Malcolm. "Never, while we have breath in our bodies, will we part with our grandchildren".

Jill was visibly shaken, but Barry was a broken man. In her agonized state she linked her hand through his arm and pressed his sleeve with light pressure, soothingly.

He automatically responded by reaching down and laying his hand over hers. He must tread gently, he thought, remain calm and collected. If he could possible avoid playing that last card up his sleeve, he would. If that ace was to be dealt, it most positively had to be a last resort.

"There is no question whatsoever of you both losing the children! As grandparents, you would still have the exact same access and rights to them that you now enjoy. The children love you - you must always be there for them".

"I know very well, Barry, what you are saying and you can talk till you're blue in the face, but the children will remain fully, I stress, fully, in our care", said Sir Malcolm as he irritatingly picked up and set down his fountain pen continually.

Barry spoke firmly but with clarity. "You amaze me Sir Malcolm, it is the ideal solution for the children and you damn well know it. I not only offer to love and cherish those children till the end of my days but will take on the full expense of their upbringing and they will be guaranteed a high standard of living".

"I am surprised at your disrespectfulness of our ability to bring up the children and I can assure you the high standard of living will be provided by us, exclusively. I have said all I am going to say on the matter, there is no way you will ever get our grandchildren. Lady Sylvia and I are wholeheartedly agreed on this matter", said Sir Malcolm, glancing quickly in Lady Sylvia's direction for her approval of his words.

She muttered her unanimity with his directive.

"I think the children's feelings on the matter should be taken into consideration. Their affection towards me is indisputable and they demonstrated unequivocally last week their close attachment to Jill", said Barry.

On the verge of losing patience, Sir Malcolm was adamant on the main point and scowled as he said, "I will not be swayed with words. I've heard you out. Give up the children? The hell, I will! Now leave!", he raised his hand and pointing to the door.

Barry looked into Jill's troubled eyes. Whether she stood by him or not when he got the children was immaterial; it was time to play his trump card.

He spoke slowly and deliberately, "The children are mine! Every single last one of them".

There was an odious shocked silence for half a minute, broken at last by the hoarse, disgusted voice of the twitching faced Sir Malcolm, "I know you love the children, Barry, that is not the issue in question, but is it worth stooping that low to get them?".

"I can assure you it is no fabrication. I have nothing in writing but I swear to God those children are mine and blood tests will prove it", replied Barry defiantly.

"I'm sorry, Barry, but why can't you accept defeat and give in gracefully without all this prevarication", said Lady Sylvia emotionally. Her eyes were red rimmed as she tried to control an overwhelming urge to cry.

"As I've said, they're mine and I'll have them should I have to go to court to get them".

Jill lowered her head and wished she was a thousand miles away. She ran her hand along Barry's sleeve until she made contact with his hand, they threaded their fingers together instinctively and she responded to the pressure of his. All eyes moved in her direction as she ventured to speak, "I am very sorry for you both, Sir Malcolm and Lady Sylvia, I am just as shocked and disappointed as you, but I do know that one child is Barry's".

"So you're in this together are you? This is despicable, I have no intention of hearing you out. You are dismissed herewith from this room and from the position I bestowed and honoured you with", was Sir Malcolm's rebuttal.

"I am very sad, for old times sake, that you are both taking this attitude. I have no option but to drag this matter through the Court of Justice", said Barry angrily.

He led Jill to the door and as they were about to leave Sir Malcolm called, "Have you thought through what a scandal would do to you, Barry? You have been known far and wide for your epitome of respectability and held in the highest regard. How will this effect your career?".

"I don't give a tinker's cuss how it effects my career", said Barry unaffected by Sir Malcolm's words.

Barry nailed Jill behind the door on entering the music room, "How come you know one of them is mine and which one?".

"The answer to the latter is Jamie; to the former, for a person to have a dimple on a certain part of their anatomy is most unusual, it would be a hell of a coincidence for another to have it on the exact same locality".

Barry smiled, "He hasn't got that, has he?".

"I'm afraid so", she replied bashfully.

"I have never proclaimed to be self righteous but does all of this matter to you, Jill? Have I shattered your illusions of me?", he asked.

"I had no illusions about you! We both love the children, what you do with your private life, past, present or future is no concern of mine".

"You're not even slightly jealous?".

"No, why should I be? What's past is past. Teresa and you; you and I; you meet a lot of exciting woman in your line of work and I'm sure you've been in and out of love many times".

"Yes, I have been in love in my day. I'm not in love with that person any more. You seem to have the impression that all these glamorous woman I clap eyes on end up in bed with me. You couldn't be more wrong! I'm not saying there aren't women around who want to bed me, simply because of who I am, but you know a man can only be tempted if he allows himself to be tempted; I have no time for it, I rarely, if ever, have time to even know their names. When I am not working I lie down and sleep and I really mean sleep alone".

She didn't like discussing sex with Barry, it brought back too many unhappy memories, but there was one area that needed resolving. "By the way, now that we are getting married, what about our pact?".

"Pact? What pact? Oh, that pact! You need have no worries on that score, you can rest assured it will remain intact". He smiled remotely, "I suppose I've become celibate now and even you couldn't raise it out of impotence", he lied. "I can't remember when I last had sex. I had given up on being married and having sex; that particular drive is the last thing on my mind, I can do without it. In a nutshell, I don't need it!".

Her thoughts were ferocious; God damn you! I can remember when I last had sex even if you can't. She should also have been asked about her feelings on the pact, after all this was a different ball game altogether. Impotent, him? Never!

While Barry and Jill were conferring in the music room, Sir Malcolm and Lady Sylvia were trying to come to terms with the predicament that had hit them out of the blue.

Lady Sylvia, as she twirled her handkerchief into a long string, watched Sir Malcolm pace non-stop. My God, she thought, our Teresa! I just can't believe it! If ever a couple were in love and got on well, it was Geoff and she, to the point of being gooey about each other. But then of course there was an article recently in a magazine in which statistics stated that many women frequently had adulterous affairs; love or sex had nothing to do with it; it was the romance they wanted, which inevitably led to sex. It was their best kept secret and that the good wife role was a fallacy imposed on them by traditional need for keeping female virtue alive.

All types of unlikely people have affairs. Perfectly decent upright people are susceptible to shocking liaisons; indeed it was a scenario that would strike a chord with numerous woman.

Then of course there was that homely woman who lived near them in Worthing; sure who would have thought it of her? The good work she had done for the community was suddenly eclipsed by rumours of her sex exploits.

She wished he would stop pacing, it unnerved her. Looking at him now with his thickening waist and balding head who would have thought that in his day women thronged after him; he had the extra advantage of being in possession of a powerful aphrodisiac, he had been a whiz-kid. Even with his hectic schedule he had time to indulge his weak streak; wine, dine and bed fascinating women. To this day he probably didn't think she knew about it - thankfully they all proved to be passing whims.

She raised the handkerchief she was twisting into a long string and bit into the end of it hard when she thought of the once when she herself lapsed; the time when he had been in Taiwan for three months. She hadn't thought of that for years and just now wished she hadn't. She sighed aloud, but in relief, that she had gone to the bother of establishing that Malcolm was in fact Teresa's father, because the liaison had been with the dashing and upstanding Colonel Thorpe, Barry's father. Yes, she hadn't thought of Charles for years.

"I don't believe the bugger! I don't believe him!", Sir Malcolm had started repeating ferociously as he paced.

"Malcolm, we would be wise to tread easily, he could be telling the truth!" , said Lady Sylvia still nibbling the end of her handkerchief.

"You mean to say you believe the bugger! That our Teresa and he had an affair! I don't know what kind of perception you are in possession of, Sylvia, but I could swear, yes swear, on a stack of Bibles, they did not".

"You can't swear to it and you know that! Who knows what goes on in other people's lives?", she said in an irritated fashion.

He was uneasy-eyed as he said, "Our Teresa was loyal to Geoff! Just like you, a loving, faithful, devoted little wife and mother".

"What are you going to do about it, Malcolm?".

"Why nothing! Nothing at all".

"He won't sit back and do nothing!".

"He'll do nothing, you'll see. He hasn't a leg to stand on!", said Sir Malcolm.

He relaxed enough to go to the window and looked down over the herb garden. Teresa had been obsessed with herbs, he thought. Barry and Jill were walking through it slowly now. Jill stooped and picked a herb and held it to her nose to sniff. He had to give Barry his due, she had proved herself to be a damn good teacher; superb, in fact. The children would miss her shockingly, but they would get over her, just as they had got over Teresa.

Jane knew something was in the air as she watched Barry and Jill walk in the herb garden, from her kitchen window. Although out of season now, on this side of the herb garden there were plantations of gooseberries, raspberries and currants, beds of strawberries and rhubarb. Then came the endless herbs, half of them never used; Teresa kept begging Jack to grow more and more for her. It wasn't the first time Jane had spied unnoticed from here. The herb garden was Teresa's favourite retreat. There was a garden seat just off the path, she would sit there and twiddle herbs in her fingers for hours. Many a time she saw her walk with Barry, stopping periodically to have an intense *tête-à-tête*, completely engrossed in each other. Occasionally they were accompanied by Geoff. On those occasions, Teresa walked between them linking arms. She didn't link when Geoff wasn't there and she never once saw Barry lay a finger on her. But there was something between them, something in the air; just as she knew there was something in the air today.

As for the children; not one of them resembled Geoff. Iain had Teresa's eyes, Alan had her gait and Jamie the colouring of... She heard the car door close and the sound of the children's excited voices. Moving the flower pot aside she leaned over and watched them run to Barry and Jill. Barry swung the excited Bonny right off her feet and held her at arms length before cradling her against him. Jill grabbed the ball from Iain and ran off with it, the boys chasing at her heels until she surrendered. Next thing she heard was Lady Sylvia calling them in; being obedient children they obeyed, but lackadaisically.

Yes, she thought, as she heard Michelle's foot steps approach, there is something in the air.

"I have this damned musical Celebrity Recital tonight; I could do without it in my present frame of mind", Barry said as he kicked a stone lying on the path in among the herbs.

"Would you like me to go?", asked Jill.

"No, I don't think it would be wise for us both to leave the children. The last thing I need now would be for them to be whipped off in a private plane. No! They need to be guarded until we get this settled".

"Barry, I can't guard them, I've been dismissed. Don't you remember?".

"I remember alright, but I'm not heeding it. After I talk to Sir Malcolm in the morning everything will be alright".

"I don't think you have grasped the seriousness of all this, they are the children's guardians and grandparents. They are not going to give them up without a fight. You'll have to take them to court to get them, as you threatened Sir Malcolm".

"In the best interest of the children it would be preferable to avoid any unnecessary publicity. If I was the only one involved, then I wouldn't give a damn".

They walked for a while both deep in thought. Jill stopped and laid her hand lightly on Barry's arm, "I'd like to go to the recital tonight, Barry !"

He looked into her blue pleading eyes and answered curtly, ''No! Not tonight".

Barry tried to put family matters behind him and relaxed in the back of the limousine. At the thought of Joanne, he grimaced as he watched obliviously through the window.

Her name hadn't been on the programme for this evening. It must have been a last minute substitution for Joan Rodgers. Both he and Joanne had avoided appearing together now for years.

It was ten years ago that they met. She was among the singers auditioning at the Royal Opera House, Covent Garden. He was looking for a soprano who could sing the lyrics to the music he had composed. He needed a voice of quality, warmth and roundness and was immediately struck by the tone and colour of her vocalization. She totally conquered him in sixty seconds flat.

To witness her at present, as a glamorous, graceful woman, one would never have envisaged her awkward, unpolished beginnings. On the plump side, one couldn't exactly describe her as beautiful; attractive would be a more apt description. She came from a family of music lovers and had been encouraged to sing from an early age; had inherited her mother's Italian looks but was a British citizen.

At that time she had worked as a semi-professional singer for about five years and although she had won competitions and had been around a number of music clubs and in operetta groups, she was clumsy and stiff, lacked sophistication and finesse. He had taken a risk choosing her but with perseverance, helped her gain confidence and stage craft, through relaxation and exercises. He accepted the credit for having been one of the most important influences in her career.

She loved the role he had chosen for her, the wit of the character and thrill of being on stage for all of a three hour production exhilarated her and she pulled it off to perfection with a voice strong in projection and expressiveness.

She had a dark allure and subtlety, could turn on a look of such powerful suggestion that it all but disabled his masculine nervous system. Over and above all the others he could have had, he chose her as a lover. She was mesmerised by his stature, no doubt, but as time passed, she acquired equal acclaim and became world famous in her own right.

Her voice was unique and reached four notes higher than normal when playing 'Luchia di Lammermoor' at Covent Garden. It had been a riveting performance and the audience held their breaths while glued to their seats.

She matured into a formidable lady with a strong will, her enigmatic hauteur shown to its best advantage; knew what she wanted and to his perplexity took the stance 'my body is my own' attitude. She became independent saying she needed no man and, as the world looked on, broke his heart.

He could remember vividly, as if it were yesterday, the last time he made love to her. It was a night of emotional passion neither of them would ever forget.

He became apprehensive as the limousine pulled up in front of 'Jury's Hotel'. The doorman opened the door and she climbed in beside him. She was a sight to gladden the eye, he had never seen her more lovely. She had been carrying a lot of extra weight when he last saw her, she stunned him now by her very slim body, her clothes oozing richness and class.

He reached over and kissed her on the cheek, her eyes shone with delight as she returned it. "Oh, Barry, please forgive me for accepting this last minute substitute part, but I felt I just had to see you again".

"I'm glad you accepted the part, Joanne, it was foolish to let our personal problems wreck the professional excellence we transmit together. The audience are in for a treat tonight", he avoided her eyes as he added, "It's almost five years since we worked together, isn't it?".

"Four years and two months since... Oh, Barry, it's been the worst four years of my life".

"How come? I may not have seen you for years but I know your every movement, as you probably know mine. You are an outstanding success and internationally renowned. What more could you want?'', he queried in amazement.

"I want... I just...", she hesitated dramatically and her eyes suddenly became red-rimmed as they filled with tears, "after you left me that night, I realized I had made the biggest mistake in my life. I have regretted it every day since".

The limousine pulled up at the Opera House. "We will discuss it later", he said dismally.

The audience went wild when they appeared together. The journalists' pounced at the entrance. "Miss Debussy, how do you feel about Dr Thorpe's engagement?".

"Dr Thorpe, how come your new fiancee isn't in the audience tonight?"

"Did you propose in Jury's before you knew Miss Debussy had been substituted for Joan Rodgers?"

"After! That is all I have to say". He pushed them aside in a show of contempt.

Joanne had more patience and spoke to one and all, "I am very happy about Dr Thorpe's engagement. Now, if you don't mind, we have come here to perform. Please let us get on with it".

Barry put his arm around her; they had been through a lot together and had an affinity unequalled. While exchanging fond looks he guided her into the theatre, at the same precise moment as the cameras flashed.

Next morning Sir Malcolm and Lady Sylvia ordered breakfast in their room. It was one duty Jane had never performed before.

Michelle had finished getting the children their breakfast, when Jill came down. There was a stampede. "Jill! Jill! Is it true you are going to marry Uncle Barry?", they all shrieked in unison.

"Yes! Yes, I'm going to marry Uncle Barry", said Jill amid the sea of happy faces.

Barry appeared round the door and got the same treatment. "When you get married, can we visit you?", Alan asked.

"I certainly hope so", said Barry raising his hands, trying to quell their excitement.

"Uncle Barry, can we come and live with you?", asked Jamie solemnly.

Michelle quickly ushered them out.

Jill carried the two plates from the stove, "My figure is on the verge of going to pot with these big breakfasts that Jane prepares".

He pushed it aside swiftly. "Just coffee for me, I couldn't face anything like that this morning".

Jill took in his fatigued appearance - but then, who wouldn't look like that if they were out to four in the morning. She thought he could have been doing with his breakfast after all the energy he must have expended in the night.

Barry ignored the paper, Jill reached over and just as she was about to pick it up, he said, "You'll have to learn to take everything you read with a pinch of salt otherwise you'll end up a nervous wreck. Not all journalism is responsible you know, a lot of it is sensational scandalizing".

The picture stared Jill in the face. Barry had his arm around the lovely Joanne Debussy. Joanne was wearing the most beautiful ocelot fur coat she had ever seen, her hands adorned with diamond rings. Jill had seen her once before at an opera in which she was the main soprano soloist. She started to read beneath the picture -

The Royal Philharmonic Orchestra, demonstrated their professionalism fully to the joy and delight of the packed house. They played Mozart Symphony No 31, Mozart Exsultate Jubilate and Mahler Symphony No 4, with Dr Barry Thorpe, composer/pianist assuming the role of conductor mounting the rostrum. Almost all composers are unable to resist this role but Dr Thorpe was remarkably efficient as he entered another world, taking the orchestra with him. Normally he dislikes all forms of showmanship, he prefers to be an almost impersonal medium between the composer, orchestra and audience rather than the central character of a drama.

Dr Thorpe delighted the audience with a final epilogue on the piano. It was composed with his own, peculiar tricks that bore his personal stamp. In many ways he is a technician as well as a great composer and artist.

It was a great night for the packed house of classical music lovers as another outstanding personality, Dame Joanne Debussy, a soprano soloist, gave an outstanding performance. She sang the song she personally made legendary, 'Wild Insatiability', the romantic and transparent music and lyrics especially composed by Dr Thorpe and Miki Delecour for Miss Debussy six years ago. Dr Thorpe accompanied her on the piano and with apparent effortless skill and vivacity, wit, warmth and vocal expertise, the brilliance of their performance shone. She bowed to the applause then was joined by Dr Thorpe who to the delight of the audience kissed her on both cheeks and holding her hand in both of his, together took a bow. It is amazing how together these two great artists gather adulation. They came, they played, they conquered. That's what the cheering, stamping packed house audience at the Opera House clearly felt. The thunderous applause went on and on.

Dr Thorpe raised his hand controlling the applause, spoke unscripted and colourfully 'of the young filly who became a pedigree Derby winner', to roars of laughter. He concluded, "I have Joanne's records and videos but there is no comparison to her beautiful live voice in the auditorium. I had forgotten how I loved that voice".

The delight these two great artists felt to be together again was obvious for everyone to see. They arrived and left sharing the same limousine.

Would she be able to cope with all this? They may get some things wrong but definitely not all.

She looked at him across the table; he was pale with black rings circling his eyes and the soft lines seemed like wrinkles today. Something was causing him enormous anguish and soul-searching. Were the children solely responsible for the way he looked this morning? How much did Joanne Debussy mean to him? Was last night simply a night of passion or with the early skirmishes behind them were they ready to fall in love again? What if Joanne Debussy decided she wanted him after all?

Jane appeared and excitedly hugged them. "I am so happy for you both, but how I'm going to miss you, Jill! As for the children, there'll be no living with them".

Barry stood up, "You'll see plenty of Jill, I promise you. Jane, will you inform Sir Malcolm that I will see him alone in his office at 10 O'Clock".

Jane went to the phone straight away, thought she had better do as she was bid. It seemed important.

She apologised for disturbing Sir Malcolm then conveyed the message.

Turning to Barry she said, "Sir Malcolm is otherwise engaged".

Two strides and he pulled the phone roughly from her hand, "You'll see me, Sir Malcolm, or you will regret it". He replaced the phone without waiting for an answer.

Jane, a devout catholic, immediately crossed herself and croaked, "Oh mercy be! Sure didn't the sacred heart fall off the wall this morning landing on my bed. It's a bad omen. Holy Mary mother of God - Let there be peace".

Barry stormed across the kitchen chiding, "Will you quit babbling rubbish woman, I've enough on my mind this morning without bad omens manifesting themselves".

As he reached the door he turned and said to Jill in an only slightly more subdued voice, "I'll see you in ten minutes in the music room".

She entered apprehensively and he told her to sit down at the table by the window. He slid a sheet of paper in front of her and asked her to read it through first then sign on the dotted line.

She had an instinctive horror of signing anything but decided at least to read it. The gist of it was that she would relinquish all rights to the children should there be either a separation or divorce. She pushed the paper towards him, categorically refusing to sign, causing an abashed silence. He had a damn bloody cheek; it was an invasion of her rights and liberties. Not only did she not like the disclaimer form one bit but it was hurtful to think that it gave reason to believe that personal trust was lacking in their relationship. It was a worrying step he had taken and she hoped that by not signing, it would be made clear to him that there was no way he would ever dominate her and that it would be the end of this type of vindictive behaviour.

"I have a moral point in imposing this contract. It would be to your advantage as much as mine leaving you free to get on with your own life if our relationship deteriorated beyond repair".

"Thank you for considering me, but I want the responsibilities to be fifty/fifty in the eventuality you have outlined". She tore up the piece of paper and left him.

Jill couldn't quell the nervous feeling in the pit of her stomach; she was worried about the children. The last thing she wanted was for the bad atmosphere to get through to them. Patrick and Michelle offered to take them to Blarney. They normally loved outings that included Patrick as he was quick witted and such fun, but they were subdued as they left. Patrick stuck his head out of the car window and called to Jill, "Don't worry, Jill, they'll have the gift of the gab when they come back".

She checked her watch every minute. How the time dragged! Barry asked her to join them in Sir Malcolm's office at 10.30. not before. It was now 10.20. She set along the corridor, wouldn't knock the door till the arranged time. Barry's voice fell clearly on her ears like an avalanche.

"You will never know the emptiness into which I was plunged. She was the love of my life, we offered each other complete happiness and joy. I am still obsessed and in love with her and will be thinking of her all of my natural life".

Jill retreated to her room like a wounded animal. She felt so exiguous and hurt on two counts. He was being disloyal to her in advertising that it was a marriage of convenience, a ludicrous charade. The other - well the other - she had to pinch herself. He promised nothing and she had hoped for nothing. She was marrying him for the sake of the children. Why was she so devastated? What made Teresa so special that he would carry a torch for her all his life? For heaven's sake the woman was dead; what did it matter if he was going to love her till the end of time. The children must always come first with her; just as they came first with him. She had to snap out of this or she would be in danger of becoming a misery guts for the rest of her life.

She looked at her watch, it was 10.32. She had to pull herself together and face the cruel ordeal. Trying to regain her dignity she took a deep breath, straightened herself and walked towards Sir Malcolm's office.

"Come in, Jill. Please sit down", said Sir Malcolm. Was the look on his face contrite or was it pity? She took the seat next to Barry avoiding his gaze.

"I'm not quite convinced yet that what you both have in mind for the children is the right thing, but I agree the only way forward is to sort it out in a level-headed way". Sir Malcolm took his seat at his desk opposite them, then almost straight away got up and started to pace. The whole episode was getting to him; this influential man in the finance world found it difficult to bear the heavy weight of his personal life.

"There is the little problem of your marriage. Is there any guarantee you will stay together?", he asked as he rubbed one eyebrow thoughtfully.

"I see no reason why we shouldn't stay together, after all Jill loves me and the children. She will be better off than she ever hoped to be; in a nutshell, I'm a good catch and I'm very fond of her. What more could she want?", said Barry.

Very fond! Thank you very much! What a - cheek! Swear words entered the vocabulary she kept inside her head, one of them she could see in asterisks; she pressed her mouth with her fingers lest they should escape through her lips. How could he? No, she wouldn't let him get to her. Without further shilly-shallying she spoke with clarity, "Our marriage will have the same chances of surviving as any other. In the event of it failing, which we hope it won't, we would work out between us what was best for the children. If we are lucky enough in being allowed to adopt the children, they will be ours equally". She stressed the word equally for Barry's benefit.

"Very well, I will talk it over with Sylvia and let you both know of our decision. In the meantime everything will continue as normal - I want no change to the children's routine".

Jill couldn't contain herself for long after leaving Sir

Malcolm's office, "So I love you, do I? I'm also after your wealth ".

"I was putting forward our case, it just might sway him".

"Yes, I suppose it would help if at least one of us loved the other".

Barry stopped and swung her round to face him. His hands gripped into her upper arms, "This marriage will be a serious commitment for both of us, we will be both honour and duty bound as a family to make it work. If you think you haven't got what it takes then for Christ sake say so now. With a special licence it can be over and done with in two weeks".

She pulled herself free and massaged her left arm which must certainly be bruised, then answered with very little enthusiasm in her voice, "We're best getting it over and done with then".

She turned on her heel and walked in the direction of her bedroom.

Sir Malcolm kept them in suspense for a further week. At his request Jill travelled to London and entered the familiar territory of the bank. She took the lift to the third floor and made her way to Sir Malcolm's office.

Miss Foster hadn't changed much, her hair was in the same neat style, her clothes impeccable but she had substituted the pearl necklace in favour of little pearl buttons on her blouse. In an assured voice she announced herself, saying, "Sir Malcolm is expecting me". Miss Foster had no alternative but to treat her courteously and declare her arrival. She got quite a bitchy little kick when Dr Barry Thorpe stepped forward to kiss her in full view of the goody-goody secretary.

When Lady Sylvia, Barry and Jill were seated, Sir Malcolm started to speak. "My friendship with you, Barry, goes back a long way. I've known you since you were knee high to a grass hopper. I am sufficiently convinced that you would fill the role, in every way, of being a good parent to my grandchildren as you have demonstrated your ability from the time of their births. We have also taken into consideration your willingness to fight for what you believe to be in the best interest of the children. However", Barry started to fidget, "Before we came to our final decision some matters had to be given further thought. We felt you might not be able to fulfil the duties expected of you, owing to your demanding career". Barry opened his mouth to protest, but with a wave of his hand Sir Malcolm silenced him while continuing, "Three months touring, two months home, is not exactly what I would call adequate time devoted to children by their father. Lady Sylvia and I, on further reflection, have decided that as you are to marry Jill, who loves you and the children passionately and by showing herself to be an able exponent of the principles needed, we are happy to have you both adopt our grandchildren".

Barry and Jill turned into each other's arms. The suspense during the long winded speech reduced them both to tears.

Lady Sylvia was also in tears as she said, "Barry the blood tests have been sent to the laboratory but regardless of whether the children are Geoff's or not, the adoption will still go ahead".

Barry composed himself and shook hands with Sir Malcolm and Lady Sylvia.

As Jill shook hands with them both, Sir Malcolm said, "We have come to love you, Jill, and apologise for offending you last week. I hope you will understand that it was only because we felt threatened".

Jill and Barry left the office happy in their new commitment. When they walked out into the street, the sun was shining. Barry rested his arm lightly around her shoulder and pressing her against him, said, "Now, a big decision! Where are we going to live?".

Chapter Six

Juggling the demands of a family of four and being the wife of a famous composer with playing the flute, did not prevent Jill Thorpe from gaining top marks in her music exam. Jill scored a distinction with her Grade 8 pass having recently resumed playing after a long break. She stopped playing at sixteen but now practices for half an hour each day, when she can find the time.

Jill's seven year old son, Jamie, also plays the flute. "He is much better than I am", said Jill, "Just a little young for exams. He is remarkable; my husband and I have high hopes for his success in the future ".

If he achieves half the success of his father, then Good Luck Jamie, you're a winner.

Jill smiled as she laid the paper aside. Barry was late, if he didn't hurry, she would have to put Bonny to bed. The nightly ritual when he wasn't touring was to take her to bed and read a story, later doing the rounds having a little chat and tucking each child in.

At the moment he was in the process of presenting an extravagant musical show to London audiences in the Prince Edward Theatre, Old Compton Street. He had been disappointed that she couldn't attend the opening night as Jamie was ill. It got a great review. He had signed up a lyricist, Miki Delecour, whom he hadn't worked with for almost five years. They worked well together and Miki came up with the emotional, dramatic dialogue while he himself composed the magnificent and mysterious rhythmical music to compliment the words.

Once when he was appearing in the Cambridge Corn Exchange doing a piano recital of his own works, she went along with him. He was a big box office draw; audiences varying from recital to recital and as Jill sat among them she could sense the wonderful ambience of anticipation. When he eventually made his appearance, he bowed then sat down to play brilliantly, as was expected of him, commanding riveted attention. His contemporary style music, pursued novelty and sensationalism and on that particular night he had been in the right frame of mind and it contained effects that surpassed even his own expectations. Watching was entertaining as his hands swept with eloquent gestures along the keys, but listening was an inspiration. The perky rhythmic figurations were unforgettable. It was a larger than life performance presented with such flair and passion and with a stimulated wildness that made the blood run faster with longing.

The sound of the genius exuded reminded her of all the beautiful things in life; champagne, chocolate and sex - her one and only experience of sex. She congratulated him as they drove home in the warm and cosy chauffeur driven limousine; he told her he had been inspired by the fact that she was in the audience. When they got home they shared a night-cap together, then she retired to her own separate room after bidding him goodnight as usual.

The chauffeur driven car drew up in the drive, Jill moved to the window. My god! She's here! The famous Joanne Debussy is here. Her name was conspicuously absent between them even though Jill knew she was appearing in his show. She had only seen her once in the flesh that time her father traipsed her across London on a cold, damp, drizzly day in January.

The woman that stepped into the room was nothing like the Joanne Debussy she remembered; that night on stage she was wearing a dress with a low cut cleavage and flaunted herself to the audience. Her father didn't seem to notice, he had been enthralled with her powerful voice. She was dressed confidently today in a bottle green suit with precision tailoring and contrasting pale green chiffon blouse. Jill felt self conscious of her own simple V-neck white cotton overshirt teamed up with casual, comfortable trousers; she was a crisp and neat, no-nonsense outfit person, found designer boutiques intimidating and only visited them when Barry wanted her to look really special. If he had warned her that Joanne was calling she would have worn something more classy.

Joanne's eyes fell straight away on Bonny, as often happened. The child was eye-catching with her beautiful head of shining black hair.

Barry said, "Jill, Joanne has a mere five minutes. She is on her way to the airport".

"I am honoured to meet you, Miss Debussy, my father is a great fan of yours", said Jill extending her hand.

Joanne stepped forward and took Jill's hand in a graceful gesture.

"Ah, you are exactly how I imagined you to be".

Her speaking voice was nothing like Jill had intuitively imagined.

Joanne took a few steps towards Bonny then said, "Where are the boys I have heard so much about them?".

"They are at a friend's house playing table-tennis, they will be sorry to have missed you", said Jill.

Bonny was ready for bed, her cheeks flushed as she hugged Bodger, her teddy. Like all children, when overtired, the slightest thing could cause irritation. She had had an exciting day. It had been her first day at dancing school. Jill had watched her proudly and was astonished at how well she had picked up the steps and only got mixed up once.

"What a little gem you are!", exclaimed Joanne and bent down and kissed Bonny on the cheek.

"I don't want you to kiss me! I don't like you!", said Bonny as she pushed Joanne's face away and ran to be picked up by Jill.

Jill was mortified and just as embarrassed as Barry, but he turned on her angrily, "How dare you let her get away with such behaviour? I thought you would have taught her better manners".

Jill, to her embarrassment, could feel the onset of a dreadful flush creep over her face. There was no excuse for his brutal and demoralising words! How could he treat her with such disrespect?

Joanne came to her rescue. "I was the one at fault. I'm not used to children, I should have known better than to kiss her".

When Joanne left, Bonny ran off to be with Jane. Jill waited, watching through the curtains, while Barry saw the crying Joanne off in the car. What she had to cry about was anybody's guess. She had a plane to catch, what a shame she wouldn't be able to have those illustrious hands fondle and explore her body tonight - have him inside her.

These corrosive thoughts drove her beyond the limit of tolerance and she unflinchingly laid into him when he reappeared. Her eyes were icy cold as they met his. "Was that necessary? I have put a lot of time and effort into creating a happy home and bringing up the children to the best of my ability. Things don't often get out of control, but when they do, the least I can expect is your backing and help in dealing with them. Regardless of your feelings towards me and mine towards you, I do not expect to be treated with contempt in front of yo... your mistress".

She watched as he glared at her in shocked disbelief; he didn't deny that Joanne was his mistress. Why the hell should he? His feelings towards herself were so minuscule she wasn't even deserving of a lie.

"I was simply trying to instil a little discipline around

here", he said quietly. "I will have no child of mine treat my friends in that fashion".

"I am not a child, it was me you reprimanded".

He looked at her with sunken, haggard eyes that had become distant before turning on his heels and leaving the room without an apology.

Jill took Bonny to bed, read to her before tucking her in for the night. The boys came back from their friend's house and spoke excitedly about how they had beaten them in a game of doubles. It was at times like this that Jill knew they missed Checkerberry and Patrick who had been a marvellous coach to them.

Barry never left the music room; the boys went to bid him goodnight and Jill overheard them repeat their excited stories.

She lay in bed unable to sleep; terrified at what had happened between them this evening. Although she had gone through a bizarre sham of a wedding knowing full well that a loveless marriage didn't exactly guarantee a bed of roses, she was a rich woman with security and stability and loved the children more than life itself. If anything threatening were to manifest itself that could separate her from them, life wouldn't be worth living.

Everything had gone reasonably smooth from the start. They bought an old crumbling mansion in Hampstead and after restoration - putting up with workmen milling around under their feet, ladders and scaffolding - it eventually, to their delight and satisfaction, became beautiful. Although it wasn't easy for her she made welcome and entertained his friends from the musical world in a most hospitable manner.

The children had settled into their new school, happy and secure. Both she and Barry had been in agreement that school wasn't just learning maths, science, English and so on, it was also about learning to get on with others. Home teaching was merely a way of protecting children from the realities of life with other people. It had been Sir Malcolm's sole idea to have the children taught at home. Barry also felt that one couldn't have a career, run a house and children all at once without one of them suffering.

Jane had been persuaded to join them in London for six months until the children settled. She was enjoying the change more than she thought possible and was only required part-time; she had her own flat and was free to come and go as she wished.

He was still playing the piano - he was renowned for his delicacy of touch as much as for his brilliance in execution. She usually loved to lie in bed listening to his musical creations that were full of imagination and spontaneity with their unquenchable sense of adventure - tonight the faint and forlorn tunes disturbed her, but eventually lulled her to sleep.

She woke with a start and her eyes widening in astonishment. Barry was sitting on her bed. He reached out and smoothed back a stray lock of hair that had fallen over her eyes when she had jumped around in alarm.

"What's the matter? Are the children alright?", she croaked sleepily.

He spoke softly, "Yes, they are alright but I'm not. I've had a lot on my mind lately but you are the last person on this earth that I should take out my pent up feelings on. I owe you an apology! You have been a magnificent mother to my children; no one could have done a finer job".

"Thank you". She lowered her head back into the pillow at the same time holding out her arm to look at her watch. "My goodness it's the middle of the night, you had better get some sleep, don't forget you have that sound track to work on in the morning".

Suddenly, without warning, he laid his head on hers; an agonizing moan escaped his lips as he buried his face in her hair that spread over the pillow. She was shocked; from the day and hour they got married he had never approached or laid a finger on her. She couldn't fault his duty as a husband in every other meaning of the word, he was better than most and a good father to the children, protecting the five of them from destructive influences.

She tentatively became shy and thought of nudging him away but tender feelings became aroused at his pitiable state. She was just about to cautiously touch his head, let him know she wanted him - feel his lips on hers, when a little hand stroked her face. She turned in amazement to find Bonny, "The big bad dragon came to ge' me and eat me up!", she said with a sob, then as her eyes became used to the darkness she saw Barry, and became bright, "Did the dragon scared you onto Jill's bed?".

Barry jumped up immediately, saying, "You and I both had a bad dream about the big bad dragon but now it has gone. Come with me, my angel, I'll tuck you in safely; no dragon is ever going to take you from us".

"After you tuck me in, Uncle Barry, I want you to come back and sleep in Jill's bed just like Mummy and Daddy".

Jill watched them disappear through the door, Bonny held tightly in his arms, laying her head affectionately on his shoulder with her legs straddled around his waist.

A few minutes later she heard him go back to his own room, then in the quiet of the night, the sound of his weight sinking into his bed. He had apologised to her, she accepted, his duty was complete. A little child's flight of fancy was not to be granted.

Jill observed Barry closely at the breakfast table. If anything an invisible wedge had come between them and he seemed to take less notice of her than any other morning. She had reservations about meeting him this morning but mightn't have bothered, the little incident in the night could almost have been a figment of her imagination. As far as his reaction was concerned, it might never have happened. To her remembrance and detriment, she knew he had the ability to have sex without love simply for physical satisfaction; she would never know what would have happened last night if Bonny hadn't disturbed them.

"Sir Malcolm wants me to fly back with him to Skibbereen this evening, I gather he has some business he wants to discuss", he said eventually.

She didn't ask what the business was likely to be, nor was an explanation offered.

Their own personal problems were never aired or discussed, neither of them offering advice or comfort to the other. She never knew what they were, but he had problems galore. The dark recesses of his past tormented him and would not go away. Every time he met up with Joanne Debussy there was no living with him, he was completely in her thrall; he stayed out all hours of the might with her and acted like a lovesick schoolboy for days until their different commissions separated them. On other occasions he was in the depths of despair probably grieving for Teresa.

Jill's main role in this marriage was to see that the children were happy, as was his. They, were both wholly obligated, putting the children before everything else. They acted out a loving relationship in front of them by occasionally kissing each other and the odd sporadic loving gesture familiar to married couples.

He stood up as he drank the last sip of tea. "I'll be off then! See you Sunday night!".

The children hadn't been wakened yet for school, if they had been he would have kissed her goodbye in turn with the rest. As it was, there was no need. She watched as he drove away.

The phone rang. Bonny had exhausted herself and had nodded off on Jill's lap. Although she was now nearly five, she still loved to be pampered occasionally.

"Maria! How are you? I am so delighted to hear you".

"Well, one of us has to make an effort and it didn't look like as if it was going to be you".

"I've been up to my eyes, Maria, but I think of you a lot", said Jill in way of apology.

"Jill, do you know what your trouble is?"

"No, but I think you're going to tell me"

"You give too much of your time to other people and not enough to yourself".

Jill held Bonny closer to her. "Maria they are family for heaven's sake".

"It doesn't make one iota of difference. You can't devote your entire life to your family. You're in the house too much, you need to get out a bit. How about coming over to my place this evening!".

"This evening?", she gasped.

"What's wrong with this evening? You've got a live-in baby sitter haven't you, or hadn't you noticed?".

"I'll think about it, expect me when you see me".

Maria opened the door and walked ahead of Jill into the sitting room. "Sorry about the chaos, I've been like this since you left".

Jill didn't see the chaos as she held out her arms to Maria.

"Hey! What's the matter with you?", said Maria cuddling her tearful friend, "If that man is causing you any misery, I'll personally knock his block in".

"No! No!", Jill answered unconvincingly.

"You should have got in touch with me, I know you're not yourself. You've changed Jill".

"I've come a long way since we were together".

"I'd like to think that I have also, but that is no reason why we shouldn't be friends, not just acquaintances".

While Maria made the coffee Jill wandered around the flat, touching little things she remembered. She had never been happy here. Thinking of him had demanded an enormous amount of her time. Looking towards the rocking chair, she thought of the many times she had rocked back and forth, moping, waiting for him to ring. She had been hopeless company for Maria, constantly in a condition of jumpiness with mood swings and couldn't eat.

"Do you love him, Jill?", Maria's voice called from the kitchen.

Jill took a few steps and she silhouetted the doorway in the dim light. "I convinced myself I didn't and that it was all for the best, but I was hiding behind a blindfold".

"You mean to say you love your husband, so what's so wrong about that?".

"Well, it's one of these open marriages: he sees other women and I'm not supposed to get jealous", sighed Jill.

"You're free to see other men, I take it!".

"Oh, I don't know about that! I certainly don't want to see other men".

"So, while he's up to it, you're supposed to remain in a state of abstinence".

Jill held the coffee with both hands as she lowered herself into the chair. "Why am I telling you all this? I'm being disloyal to my husband".

"No, Jill, look upon it as therapeutic, it wasn't good for you keeping this bottled up. What are friends for if they can't lend an ear and a shoulder to cry on". She filled up their coffee cups, "I know it isn't proper for me to give advice but I'm going to give it anyway - seduce him".

It was 12.15am when Jill put her key in the lock. A door immediately opened and Jane came scurrying out to meet her.

"Oh, Jane, I am so sorry for keeping you out of your bed, but the traffic was dreadful".

"Don't you worry a hair about that. The children have slept like tops - but that woman has been here!", she said uneasily.

"What woman?".

"That high class singer. She rang first; I told her you weren't in, then I got the shock of my life when she turned up regardless".

"Joanne Debussy! What did she want? She was supposed to have flown off somewhere yesterday and anyway she knew Barry wasn't here".

"God knows what she wanted! I made her a cup of tea, then she asked me if she could have a look at the children to pass time till you came home, but I wasn't having any of that. I just told her straight that they might wake up and get frightened. She left soon afterwards saying she would get in touch with you again".

Jill tried to keep her voice unperturbed, "I dare say we will find out what it is all about when she rings. You go off to bed now, I'm sorry I kept you up".

Jane stopped at the door. "She asked if you went out often. I told her you rarely if ever went out and that you had gone to visit a girl friend. I got the feeling she didn't believe me".

"Oh, well", Jill shrugged, "I don't care what she thinks".

"Indeed", said Jane as she went into the hall, "What's it to do with her?".

"I have discovered that on the day the twins were born, you set up a trust fund for them. Likewise on the birth of Jamie and Bonny", Sir Malcolm spoke guardedly.

"Yes, that is correct! I know you set Geoff and Teresa up here in Checkerberry when they got married but it takes a lot of money to keep up a place like this and they weren't exactly in a position to do that on a G P's salary. I had more money than enough, they didn't want anything from me but I insisted on organizing the trust funds and that they drew out enough to cover all the children's expenses such as holidays and schooling for the twins. I asked for nothing in return''.

Sir Malcolm began his nervous little habit of picking up and setting down his fountain pen. He knew what he had to say would probably shatter Barry but he felt obligated to divulge his chance discovery.

"Why did you set up the trust fund for Bonny?".

"Why not? What I did for one had to be done for all of them", Barry retorted quizzically.

"The three boys are yours, Barry, but Bonny has a blood group different to Geoff, Teresa and yourself".

Barry was about to protest when Sir Malcolm pushed a piece of paper containing the evidence under his nose.

He read the laboratory reports over and over in a state of shock, then lowered his ashen, grief stricken face into his hands in devastation. He would have some explaining to do to Sir Malcolm but for now he had only one question in his mind; who in hell's name was Bonny's father. How could she do this to him? How the hell could she do it?

Barry arrived home late Sunday night. When Jane went back to her own flat, Jill at last had time to take note of his haggard appearance.

"I need to talk to you, Jill". He flopped into the chair.

Jill knew that she had wasted her time by putting her hair into a French pleat. She had also pulled out a few wispy tendrils to fall softly around her face in the hope of generating sexual vibes.

He simply avoided looking at her and she knew he was in no fit state to talk about anything tonight, never mind pick up sexual vibes. She was curious to know what he had to tell her but said, "Leave it till tomorrow, have a good night's sleep first; you're shattered".

"You're right", his expression showed obvious relief as he dragged himself out of the chair again. "Goodnight! We will talk in the morning".

She watched his slouched figure disappear through the

door as she plumped up the cushions. If he doesn't get himself together, his work will suffer.

She lay in her bed, tossing, turning and flinging while fighting her overwhelming craving to have him as a lover combined with a need to comfort him. In despair she sank down into the bed and curled up in the foetal position. "Please God, rid me of this longing..."

She sat up suddenly; he's in the next room for God's sake and he was her husband, what did it matter if he didn't love her, she loved him - why should her longings be futile? Charged with a creative energy she swung her legs out of the bed and went to him.

He was in a drugged sleep and hadn't put the lid back on the bottle. She read the label 'do not exceed one'. Tipping the tablets out she counted them. He had taken three. Three shouldn't do any harm, perhaps knock him out quicker and for longer. Climbing into the space at his back, she put her arm around him protectively and snuggled close against him beneath the duvet. She felt no sexual passion, just complete and utter contentment; of all the exotic locations in the world, this was the only place she wanted to be. Succumbing to a heavenly feeling of relaxation, one more breath and she would have been asleep, then as if he was a million miles away she heard Jamie's voice. "Uncle Barry, I want a drink and Jill's not there".

"Quiet, Jamie, Barry is asleep, I'll take you".

She stopped just long enough to check Barry's

temperature, her cheek against his forehead. Satisfied he was sleeping more peacefully, she left him.

She busied herself clearing up the breakfast things, wondering what would have happened if he had woke up and found her in his bed. Would there have been an immediate overwhelming mad passion betwe.. ?

"Sit down Jill! There is something I need to tell you".

His stooped form stood by the window, hands deep in his pockets, he waited for her to be seated before speaking.

"Bonny is not my child! I was tricked into thinking she was. It's a long story but she isn't Teresa's either; Joanne Debussy is her mother and she wants her back".

His voice shook as he told her the incredible story of how Teresa and Geoff acquired Bonny and of the night she was born.

Chapter Seven

Patrick drove through the night, his destination the Mosel region. He chose his wines carefully for specific palates, sampling every wine he imported. The most expensive wines will not necessarily please every palate - only last week Michelle spat a fine wine in his face, saying it reminded her of a wheelbarrow full of rotten leaves.

As he thought of Michelle, he shifted uneasily in the seat; he wished she was less of a ditherer. He had proposed marriage to her some seven months ago when Barry and Jill got hitched, knowing that women can become envious when their friends beat them to it, but no, she wouldn't commit herself. It had upset him when she declined his offer and took up another position with the McGurkin's, hardly having time to wipe the dust of the Webb's from her feet.

They had been lying lazily on the grass by the ruins of an old castle at Galley Head, his hand idly playing with strands of her hair. "Let's not be hasty; marriage is a big step, anyway I don't know whether you love me enough!", she had answered him pensively.

"I wouldn't ask you if I didn't love you for Christ sake", he chided sulkily, smarting from her rejection of him.

"I don't want to have a barney with you, Patrick, but we've grown on each other and have become a habit; you have a house and want children. I won't marry anyone just to fill a void".

Patrick inherited a small estate from his parents and although modest in size, it held a certain prestige.

"If I could prove to you that I love you, would you marry me?".

She averted her gaze, pulled a blade of grass and gnawed it between her teeth. "I don't know, Patrick! I just don't know! I know I'd be heart-broken if I couldn't see you again. It's just..".

"So what you're actually trying to tell me is, you don't know if you love me enough either. I wish I could penetrate that pretty little head of yours and stamp on your mind that we love each other. Not only do I love you, Michelle, but I think we are ideally suited. We have the same background and aspirations". He paused somewhat, then reaching across the grass found her hand and they intertwined their fingers. "Do you know what I think is wrong with our relationship?".

"What?". She pulled herself up on her elbow and looked earnestly down into his eyes, eager to know. There was no doubt about it, she wanted things to be right between them.

"I think your obsession in being a virgin on your wedding night is ruining everything else that is good between us".

They enjoyed an affectionate and loving relationship but with a sexual barrier.

"Oh, Patrick, you've got it all wrong! Honestly! I know I

will only go so far but it's not because I'm obsessed with being a virgin, its simply that my hypothesise is: that love and sex go hand in hand. When I'm certain that I love you then I won't give a damn about being a virgin on my wedding night".

He laughed as he pulled her over on top of him, "When you're ready and getting those shivers running up and down your spine, let me know. In the meantime, give me a great big sloppy French kiss".

She thumped him. "Oh, Patrick O'Rafferty".

He raised himself so that she fell off him with light thud onto the grass - they wrestled and laughed together while he tickled her ribs - as her spasmodic laughing decreased he tentatively ran his hands sensually down over her breasts but she suddenly jumped up saying, "Heaven's above! Look at the time it is?".

There was no way he would ever come on heavy or try to coax her beyond the point she wanted to go. He surprised even himself at times; his sexual drive was perhaps just bordering on the lower edge of moderate.

Patrick met her through the Webb's. They were a delightfully friendly couple and good customers from they first came about the place. Geoff had been a big wine drinker and the delectable Teresa, when coaxed, liked a sweet auslese.

Teresa called Michelle to the kitchen and asked her to sample the wines for the staff. She was like that, Teresa, always wanting to please everyone, a thoroughly genuine, loving, kind lady.

Patrick recalled teasing Michelle by saying to Teresa, "Where have you been hiding this golden girl?".

Teresa laughed at Michelle's blushes, then decided to play cupid. "I'll leave you to it and if you have any sense, Michelle, grab him while the iron's hot, you couldn't go far wrong with Patrick; nobody could".

Yes! A proper lady was Teresa.

He and Michelle took to each other instantly and he didn't have to do much coaxing for her to accept that first date. Luckily he was fond of children as Michelle, at times, insisted on having them on tow. He had a way with children and they loved his antics; yes, he appreciated he was due some credit for the way in which those children came through that tragic time in their lives unscathed.

Patrick had plenty of time to think and threw back his head and laughed when he thought of how he had coached the two older boys to play table tennis to the extent they could almost hammer him now. Alan got so good at his forehand drive and played it with a lot of top spin that Patrick, very often, couldn't return it.

Once Alan and Iain were playing for Patrick's old bat which he had used to win the Bantry Junior Championship, when he was fifteen. Alan was leading 9-3 when Iain embarked on new tactics. He stood further back from the table, his chop shot began to work and the ball dropped just over the net. The score was 14-10 with Alan leading and his turn to serve. Iain played a waiting game - said he had a fly in his eye, but none could be found. Then he fiddled around with his socks and untied his laces to do them up tighter. When they eventually started again Alan tried to speed things up but made silly mistakes. Iain wouldn't be hurried and carried on at his slow speed to win 21-19. It was such a close thing that Patrick decided they should share the bat.

Night-time driving was both tedious and tiresome. It wouldn't be long till he got into grapevine country. He became invigorated; this place never failed to give him a buzz.

At last Patrick pulled up at his destination; it was beginning to get light. He got out of the car and stretched to the delightful bird song, which was music to the ear. How he loved it here in the valleys of the Mosel. There was a nip in the air; he hoped the late frost wouldn't kill off the young shoots and ruin the year's wine.

There were eleven wine growing regions in Germany, the most northern wineyard area in Europe, where much research had been done to develop the hardy grape varieties that can survive the low temperatures most of the time.

He went to the little shed and found the key hanging under a towel that Frau Wedikind had left out for him. He would try and get a few hour's kip before starting the rounds of the vineyards.

No late lie-in for Patrick; he stepped out into the clear sharp air of the morning raring to go. He drove towards his first port of call which was a small family owned vineyard.

The breathtaking splendours of the countryside gladdened his heart. The scenery here was superb with the slopes covered over with the young vine leaves, the sun's rays reflecting off them and lighting up an otherwise tranquil and relaxing scene. It had been harvesting time when he was last here in October; warm days, cool nights with a heavy dew. At that time the loaded carts came back from the vines, the pickers sang as they followed. Skill and endless labour had made the harvest possible - now he was going to taste the wine.

As he pulled in, the vineyard owner and his wife came to greet him. "Good Morning, Pat, how very nice to see you again".

"It's a great pleasure to meet you both again also", said Patrick shaking hands zealously first with Karl Heinz, then Frau Braemer, his wife.

They went inside and the two sons of Karl Heinz joined them, Franz and Rudolf. They all congregated round a large table - Patrick was eager to get on with the business of tasting last year's output together with the more mature vintages, but before this crowd got down to business they enjoyed nothing more than a joke or two to enliven the tone of things. Thankfully this was the only family that went in for this type of thing or he would still be sampling wine at midnight. He endured their wry humour and joined in when they laughed heartily at their own jokes. Franz had quipped, "I hear they are as Irish as Patrick Murphy's pig in Cork and that every Tom, Dick and Harry is called Patrick".

Rudolf's contribution was: "One old man asked an other old man, 'How long is it since you made love to a woman? The old man thought long and hard before replying, 'I suppose it was 1935'. 'My God', said the first old man, 'That's an awful long time ago'. The second old man looked at his watch and said, 'It's not that long ago, sure it's only 19.59 now'".

Patrick gauged the tone of his jokes according to whether Frau Braemer joined them or not. Today she joined them.

"Did I ever tell you the one about the biggest womaniser in Bantry?".

Their eyes lit up in readiness for the punch-line before the onset.

"Well", said Patrick, "The womaniser's wife had good reason to be suspicious and jealous as every night, when he was supposed to have been out with his friends for a few jars, he came home with long female hairs, in various shades, on his jacket. One Saturday night after scouring him for alien strands and discovering he was as clean as a whistle, his wife started to scream recriminations at him. "Sure I always knew you'd go with anythin' in a skirt, Shamus O'Leary, I see you've even taken to bald women".

Patrick gave Karl Heinz and his family more than ample time to roar with laughter then promptly encouraged them to get down to some serious business.

Ten fine wine bottles were dutifully opened. It lent to a very friendly atmosphere as Frau Braemer served everyone with more generous than necessary measures.

This crowd must get half cut every day, Patrick thought, as they guzzled the wine for no good reason but to keep him company. No such luxuries for himself though, there was no way he could start drinking at this early hour; he wanted to be able to stand at the end of the day and remember what the first wine tasted like.

He held the glass up to the light checking for tartrate crystals. In Germany these are regarded as signs of distinction but it was harder to convince the foreign customer. Perfectly good wine had been returned to Patrick in the past - customers thinking they were glass splinters.

White wines with a green tinge are usually very young and, in general, the older the white wine the deeper its yellow colour becomes.

With great gusto and skill he swirled the wine around in the glass, smelt it, then slowly covering his tongue fully to arouse his taste buds enabling him to test the flavour and vibrancy. He then spat into the spittoon; that wasn't the end of it - he waited for the aftertaste.

Patrick would register his approval of a good wine with a

slight raising of an eyebrow or a gentle nod, his diagnosis carried authority. His motto was, if the fruit of the wine was properly balanced with alcohol, acids and tannin, a wine would develop its finesse and elegance. These people seemed to get it right year after year.

He listed a few of the light, crisp and refreshing wines which he knew would go down well in his area and a few of the sought after good quality fine wines that were carefully matured in these small estates.

The party eventually broke up and Karl Heinz offered him a full glass. "This wine is one of our specialities. Try it, Pat! I know you'll like it and down the lot this time".

He was about to raise the glass to his lips when he saw her. He held his breath as he became rooted to the spot - every nerve in his body clamped as he stared at her - she stared back with keen searching eyes; eyes that seemed to search into the very depths of him. She became embarrassed at his equally intensive gaze and lowered her baffled, probing eyes.

Karl Heinz's voice in his ears brought him out of shock. "I have seen some admiring looks at my assistant but this cops the lot". He gestured for the girl to join them. "Helga! Come and meet Pat O'Rafferty", he spoke in German.

The girl moved closer, smiled and said, "Guten Morgen".

"Guten Morgen. Sprechen Sie Englisch?", Patrick enquired as he held out his hand to her.

"Yes, a little", she answered putting her hand in his.

He had shook this hand many times, the slender fingers gripped his with a familiarity well known to him.

She moved away in her habitual gait, having dutifully expressed a few pleasantries, to deal with another wine taster. How the hell did she get into this setup? Her voice drifted with assured authority to his ears; "Good news for vegetarians is that a litre of red wine contains up to six milligrams of iron. Scientists are puzzling over recent medical findings that imbibing red and white wine has been found to offer protection against heart disease, stress and serves to ward off the misery of the common cold".

Why, she hadn't known a damn thing about wine, she sounded technically proficient now; could probably teach him a thing or two.

"How long has Helga been with you?", asked Patrick, trying to come over casual.

Karl Heinz looked in her direction and his eyes softened as he answered. "I suppose it's coming up on fifteen months now. I'm surprised you haven't seen her before; you may have missed her though as she works part-time. She got herself involved with some goddamn son-of-a-bitch who beat the daylights out of her. We took her in for her own safety and she has proved to be a valuable asset to us. That woman has a fair business head on her shoulders; increased our sales at a hell of a rate. Hey, Pat! Never knew you were a womaniser. I thought you came here to order wine not goggle over my staff".

"I'm not normally; but by jove she's a stunner!". He had to work out his next move and wondered what the hell he was going to do! There was no question about it - there was only one thing to do: "Damn! I've just remembered something! I need to get through to my office. Do you mind if I make a phone call?".

Karl Heinz led him through to the back. The small desk was cluttered with order books and wine manuals. He pointed to the phone, "There you are Pat, go ahead", and left him.

Patrick began dialling the English code; she entered the small office, sorted through some manuals then whispered to him, "Please excuse me". Selecting one of the manuals, she smiled and left.

It was ringing out; a female telephonist at the other end of the line spoke to him. He hesitated; she spoke again; without pausing to consider the consequences, he replaced the hand-piece without uttering a word. All hell would break loose once he imparted his message. No! He would see how the land lay with her and work on instinct; maybe she didn't want to go back. He shuddered at the thought.

He picked up his wine glass and went in search of Karl Heinz. Patrick had to meet that girl again; perhaps he could do some petty blackmailing.

"Right, Pat, have you made up your mind what you will need this year?", said Karl Heinz opening up the order book.

"I'll increase my order, Karl Heinz, on the condition that you fix me up a date for tonight with that dish", he nodded in Helga's direction.

"You're a good customer, Pat, and that sounds tempting, but if I though you had anything immoral on your mind, I'd do without the order", said Karl Heinz steadily.

"I know you're an honourable man, Karl Heinz, but then you know the same of me. If I wanted a piece of skirt, which I can assure you is the last thing on my mind, I'd go out on the town. No! I genuinely want to take that girl out for a drink and a chat. I'll have her back at 10.30 sharp".

Karl Heinz gave in subserviently. "That's if she goes! She's not one for dates. Right I'll have a word with her".

Karl Heinz moved off while Patrick tasted the wine with wandering attention; he watched them confer together then Karl Heinz took the puzzled girl by the elbow and marched her in his direction.

"Right Pat! Take the corner table! Do your own dating!".

He had sat across the table from her many times before, but never had she stared at him with such cool, blank eyes.

"Helga, I would be more than pleased if you would join me for a drink tonight", said Patrick, hoping she would take him at face value.

She continued to stare blankly as she spoke. "I'm sorry, Mr O'Rafferty, I don't fraternise with the customers".

"Look! Karl Heinz can vouch for me! I'm not after your body, I've got a perfectly lovely girl friend at home. I have four days and nights in this area and I would be glad of someone my own age to have a chat and a drink with now and again. If I look as if I am going to lay a finger on you, then you can hoof it without a backward glance. How's that?".

She seemed to become more intrigued than anguished, "What part of Ireland do you come from, Mr O'Rafferty", she asked with a half-smile.

"Call me Pat! I'm from... ", he hesitated and ventured cautiously, "Bantry, County Cork", said Patrick his eyes searching deep into hers for a glimmer of recognition.

"Alright! Don't call for me before 8 O'Clock, I'm not one for dressing up so I'll need time to search out something to wear".

She promptly moved off behind the rows of filled, well defined and catalogued wine racks and disappeared.

Patrick raised his glass containing Karl Heinz's particular speciality, deciding it was intriguingly rare with a distinctive flavour, he said, "As well as my usual order, Karl Heinz, I'll have a pallet of this spatlese. It's vibrant and fruity, a damn fine wine!".

Although Patrick had frequented this area for years, he had never known about this little hide-away Helga directed him to which was hidden by the hills. Before entering he stopped to admire the magnificent view and breathe in the healthy fresh air. What a beautiful peaceful place to be, he thought, as he watched a boat snake it's way down the winding Mosel river.

They settled into a secluded corner in the Weinstuben. Patrick asked her what she would like to drink.

"Although I work at the vineyard, Pat, I rarely, if ever, drink. I enjoy observing other's enjoyment of the many wines that are pressed, fermented and matured in the cellars".

Patrick preferred Halbtrocken wine but ordered a bottle of Trittenheimer, an elegant auslese made from riesling grapes in one of the best estates in the Mosel.

When the order arrived he poured a small amount into her glass, "Try a few sips, you'll like this one!".

She raised the glass to her lips cautiously; the same lips that had savoured it so many times previously and on the first sip she smiled unbelievably and said, "I like it, Pat! Do all Irish wine importers have an extrasensory gift of perception enabling them to match up particular wines to particular people?".

"I wish it was as easy as that; no we're not all elf-like". said Patrick laughing as he tilted the bottle and filled up her glass.

"I would like to know all about you and your life in Ireland".

He filled her in with background information as best he could. "Ireland is a land of charm where the people are kind and friendly and the landscapes range from beautiful to more beautiful. County Cork has a wild and wonderful beauty that defies description. The town of Cork", he broke into song, "That stands on the banks of my own lovely Lee". She loved music; he'd tell her about the music. "A bit of fiddle and harp music, Irish dancing and sing-song, is what they go in for there, often in the most out-of-the-way places. It is the home of the Irish National Ballet and has its own Opera House; big names come there Bar... and sure Michael Jackson visited the Cork Stadium last year.

"Then there's Blarney Castle, four miles to the north of Cork. It is set in superb landscaped gardens. When Cormac MacCarthy had the castle built in the mid-fifteenth century, he certainly meant it to last. The walls are more than three and a half meters thick at the base, in solid stone - every last one had to be hauled manually from local quarries. The famous Blarney stone is set high up in the castle walls - I took four children there - once they kissed it, they nearly drove me mad with their perpetual gab".

"I take it you've kissed it then, Pat! You appear to me as if you could sweet-talk your way in or out of anything".

They smiled at each other.

"It sounds exciting there", she said with a far away look in her eyes.

He could scarcely take his eyes off her face. Her skin was like velvet and her eyes wide and bright as a child, her black hair tied back in a pony tail. She looked so young for her age - could pass for someone in their early twenties, but Patrick knew different.

"Hey! Enough about me, I want to hear about you. Tell me about yourself?".

The warmth she had been radiating disappeared as if it had never been and when she spoke he detected the indignation in her voice. "My past is my own! I like to keep it to myself! The Braemer's respect that wish and I don't want to speak of it to anyone".

Patrick moved his hand across the table and touched hers fleetingly. "I will respect your wish also".

He had to get the warmth back into those eyes and knowing she was no stranger to his wisecracks, nobody loved them more than she so he proceeded to tell her about a farmer from Glengarriff ringing him. 'Come on over Patrick, we're having a wake and bring us a case o' somethin'. I answered him, 'I dunno now - I've a bad case of laryngitis'. The farmer came back with, 'What the hell; sure this lot'll drink anythin'."

He waited for her response - she never batted an eyelid.

She sipped her wine then lifted her eyes to meet his gaze

calmly, "Tell me another one Pat! Sure I've heard that one".

Patrick held her gaze in amazement; it was a true story that he had jazzed up for customers. Suddenly his memory jolted - why, he had told her himself and as he gazed into her eyes he became lost in exquisite nostalgia. She was wearing a seductively slinky green dress that evening; how it clung to her curves. She was forever stylish and clothes looked exceptionally good on her. There was no such expense in the rig she was wearing tonight; a plain blue dress with simple lines that moulded to her figure. He was a bust man, noticed them first - she had a magnificent bust, tiny waist and rounded hips, ideally proportioned. This girl didn't need all those expensive clothes that she used to wear - she was a natural and would look well in a sack.

Her voice brought him back to the present. "Pat, please don't stare at me, it's frightening".

On the drive back through the hills Patrick sensed that she was not altogether at ease with him so decided to speak of Michelle. "My girlfriend is a nanny! Looks after other people's children. The family she is with at the present time have had more than their fair share of troubles. The young mother died while giving birth and the father was left with only an ageing mother to cope with the two children. It suited Michelle to take over as she was between jobs and of course she loves the little nipper that never knew her own mother".

"Oh how tragic! Your Michelle must be a wonderful

person to do a job like that", said Helga.

"Yes, she is - wonderful", said Patrick tenderly.

"I feel safe with you, Pat, now that I have heard you talk so lovingly of your girlfriend".

"Why? Did you not feel safe before?".

"I did, Pat", she said as she laid her hand on the sleeve of the arm that held the steering wheel.

He reached his other hand over and laid it on hers for a few seconds, in an intimate gesture.

He deposited her back safe and sound on the dot of 10.30, eliminating any need for anxiety by Frau Braemer and was about to ask when he could see her again when she said, "How long did you say you were staying in the area, Pat?".

"Four days! But I'm my own boss, I can stay longer should the need arise".

"I hope a need arises so that you will stay longer. You are the first person I have been out with since I arrived here".

"Ah, sure I'm honoured, sure I am", said Patrick exaggerating his Irish accent, with a twinkle in his eye.

"You have an honest face! I like you, Pat O'Rafferty", she said coyly and moved towards the Braemer's door.

"Hi! When am I going to see you again?"

She stopped and turned - the moonlight caught her eyes; they were alive and flirtatious. Was this the way she charmed the two men in her life? What right had he to call him a bastard from now on? Sure he had an affinity with him. He wanted this girl!

"See you tomorrow night, Pat O'Rafferty. Same time!".

He watched as she disappeared behind the Braemer's door and was fully aware of the very weak streak that had developed within him with regard to her. His sexual urge was bordering on the excessive.

Frau Wedikind was having a nightcap and asked Patrick to join her. He liked her, she was small, plump and friendly; he was a favourite with her and he damn well knew it.

"How was your date with Helga, Pat?", she asked as she poured him a large measure.

"Terrific!", answered Patrick. "How well do you know the girl?".

Frau Wedikind's face acquired a grave sadness. She downed a large mouthful, then another, before answering. "I have known her since Karl Heinz brought her out of hiding and a very nice, pleasant person she is. She came to them begging, her clothes in tatters with neither shoes on her feet nor a handbag in her possession. When they asked her if she would like a bed for the night she fell at their feet and worshipped them. Badly beaten she was! A deep gash on the back of her head and wouldn't let them see her body as it was too badly bruised. He must have given her a hell of a thrashing because she had no idea how long she had wandered about, sleeping rough on the embankment of the river and sheltering under an old iron bridge, while surviving on grapes and apples. She had been continually chased by people who, from her unkempt appearance, thought she was a gypsy or a destitute alcoholic and whore. Karl Heinz and his wife wanted her to report the animal who had treated her so viciously but she wouldn't. They think she was afraid he would find out where she was and come after her again.

"Once she got well, she volunteered her services and has been there ever since".

Patrick couldn't bear it, he dropped his head in both hands and squeezed his lids tight together to suppress the tears that were battling to get out.

"Don't worry your head about it, Pat, it's all behind her now, the Braemer's love her and she is happy as the day is long".

He won the battle, stood up and blew his nose.

Patrick had work to do and vineyards to call on. With visiting, tasting and ordering, he never knew four days to pass so quickly. He made a couple of trips out of the Mosel to check out recent vintages from other favoured regions. He liked the distinctive flavour of Nahe wines and gave a sizeable order to one of the large efficiently run Cooperatives. The day he spent in the Rheingau reminded him of how lucky he was to be able to taste some of the most elegant, smoothest and finest wines in the world. On these trips he always bought a few pallets of choice estate bottled wines - Erzeugerabfullung, from old friends near Erbach and in the delightful village of Keidrick. He assumed the language of wine: superb bouquet; full of light and charm; fruity, spicy and well rounded; delicate with finesse; sturdy with backbone. He was of the opinion that whatever fell from his tongue could describe a wine and make or break somebody's day.

If she left his mind for half an hour at a time it was the height of it. The highlight of his existence was picking her up each evening and knowing she was thrilled to be in his company.

The Braemer's dropped the 10.30 deadline after the first night. "I could stay out all night with you now for all they care - of course I wouldn't want to", she had said with a glint, or was it a hint, in her eye?

Patrick had arranged earlier in the week that he would stay on for a fifth day and as Helga had a day off he invited her to spend it with him in the Rhine district.

It was his fourth night and up to the present he had never laid a hand on her.

They walked along the deserted riverbank; she slipped her hand into his and he drew her to a stop, facing him. Patrick wouldn't have known how to go about seducing the lady of old, nor would he have wanted to; she was top-notch and a socialite, but Helga was a different kettle of fish. This little more than peasant girl was delightfully approachable. They faced each other in the moonlight.

"Helga, has anyone ever told you how exquisite you look in the moonlight?".

She giggled. "I should think not. Sure who but yourself, Pat O'Rafferty, would be daft enough to tell me a thing like that".

"Do you think I'm daft wanting to kiss you?".

"If you are daft enough to want to kiss me, then I'd be daft not to, and do you know something? You and I were meant to kiss sooner or later and I vote very much for sooner".

It was at times such as these when they were so like-minded that he was sure they were made for each other.

They went into each other's arms and experienced the delights of a first kiss that was long overdue. Their lips sweetly locked together while she ever so lightly caressed the front of his chest; he felt her teeth, ran his tongue up and down across them, then in and in...

For the time being Michelle was forgotten - they kissed again and again as if there was no tomorrow, he didn't want to let this girl out of his arms.

"Oh Pat, how am I going to be able to let you go?".

He pressed her body closer to him. "I'll come back often". His words were light but his heart heavy.

She spoke impulsively, "Take me with you, Pat! How I'd love to see those places you've told me about".

The words hit him like a ton of bricks. He could never take Helga home - never.

She ran her hand down the front of his body in a way Michelle would never have done. Michelle had never been fully awakened sexually, she was too inexperienced to recognise the sensations of sexual provocation - but Helga, whether she knew it or not, was a married woman with desires; kissing wasn't going to satisfy her. Would any man in his right senses be able to resist her? He was going to do just that because one thing he knew for certain was that she had to be protected from pregnancy, at all costs, and he wasn't prepared to-night.

He ran his hand down and placed it on top of hers. A sigh of pleasure escaped his lips as he pressed her hand against him, savouring the glorious feeling till he could endure it no longer, then quickly removed her hand from the bulging aroused part of his anatomy. He drew her palm to his lips, kissing it continuously, while their hearts thumped loudly together in unison.

"Time we were in the land of nod girl, we have an early start towards the Rhine valley in the morning".

"Oh, Pat O'Rafferty! Pat O'Rafferty!", she wailed against his chest.

The Braemer's came out to wave them off, they had never seen Helga look so radiant. She was wearing her new floral dress with a scooped neckline that fell exquisitely over her striking figure. Frau Braemer had insisted that she took a loan of her necklace as it matched to perfection. They liked Pat O'Rafferty, he was a decent sort, but he was going home tomorrow. How was the girl he left behind going to take it? God only knows!

They visited a wine fair with stands set up in the cobbled streets between the half-timbered houses. Wine could be bought by the glass; one didn't have to buy in bulk - this fair was for everyone. There was singing and dancing in the street amidst the aroma of barbecued sausages and chickens. Helga was no stranger here, she knew a lot of the people that had visited the Braemer's vineyard. She continually stopped to speak to friends introducing them to Patrick. He couldn't keep up; German names went in one ear and out the other.

Further along there were market stalls, laden with everything one could think of. "I want to buy you something Helga! What do you want?"

"Oh Pat, as far as I can remember no one has ever bought me anything in my life". She was happy and sad at the same time.

You are so wrong, my baby, he thought. Someone had showered her with exquisite gifts. He was forever buying for her; and giving, giving, giving - one baby, two babies, three babies, four and if he had access to her - five babies, six... Damn! The man wasn't worth getting het up over -

today Helga was his.

He bought her a silver charm bracelet for luck; it hadn't been expensive but her eyes shone with delight.

They walked through the market, impressed by the sheer quality and variety of the fruits and vegetables for sale; pale green asparagus, dark green artichokes, their leaves tipped with violet. Every so often she would lift her arm to admire the bracelet and jingle it about, their smiling eyes would meet and she would drop her head bashfully on his shoulder.

Alas, all good things had to come to an end; some importers ordered straight from wine fairs but Patrick wanted to visit the vineyards and cellars.

The rest of the day passed quickly. Helga was an expert and without tasting one wine was able to explain to him that the wines of the Rhine are fuller, smoother, rounder and fruitier than that of the Mosel. "They taste more like peaches than apples", she said. She couldn't have been more accurate.

As the early evening approached he looked anxiously at his watch. She noted his glance, laid her hand on his arm and said, "Pat, I want to stay here with you tonight!". It had been going through his mind all day. He had high hopes of her making a full recovery; how would they feel about it afterwards? But, for now, he was desperately in need of her. "What about the Braemer's?", he asked.

"They're only a phone call away".

Frau Wedikind was only a phone call away also.

They booked into the Hotel Krone, near Assimanshausen. These hoteliers also owned their own vineyards and produced an unusual red wine. They were very friendly people and recognized Helga instantly, but acknowledged the sensitivity of the occasion and dealt directly with Patrick in a business-like manner.

They had a meal in the restaurant. The hoteliers had never known Helga to radiate such happiness as she did tonight in the company of this zealous Irish man. He told her jokes continually as if his main reason for living was to make this girl laugh and be happy.

His naked form slipped into bed beside her. "What's this?", said Patrick as he ran his hands over the body concealed by a silk slip. For one so keen to get him to bed she was remarkably modest and inhibited in baring her body.

Likewise she ran her hand sensually over his naked body, displaying no signs of shyness. "You'll have me with my slip or not at all, Pat O'Rafferty".

He had seen her in a bikini on the beach and even with four children, she still had the attributes of a teenage girl.

He didn't like the damned ultimatum one little bit but gathered her into his arms - he was confident the slip would come off before the night was through.

"Pat, I want to make love with you very much, but not just yet. You see, I get these dreadful headaches and all the excitement of the day has brought one on.

Just his luck, first the slip, now of all the doggone times to have a headache.

Nothing could, however, allay the joy of holding her in his arms. He sought her mouth with his and ran his tongue along the curve of her teeth. She bit into him; he liked it.

"Pat, I've never told anyone this before but I am not really hiding my past, its just - I haven't got a clue about it - there are some things though, that I could describe to the last leaf. There's a herb garden and I know where everything is. There's a seat beside the herb garden; it is green. Most of the time I have only flashes of places and faces that are unfamiliar to me; and dreams - I am tortured by terrifying nightmares; then I wake up to the reality of nothingness".

Patrick became overly alert. "What are these frightening dreams about?".

"Lots of strange people and strange places. When I first set eyes on you, Pat, I thought you were one of the faces in my dream, but obviously you've never met me before or you would have said. Very often there is a little girl; a beautiful little girl with jet black hair. She appears to be playing happily among my favourite herbs; then when I hold out my arms to her, she backs off. She doesn't know me and becomes frightened. I get so angry and I chase after her, then when I catch her - I wake up. My heart pounds and I am so full of guilt that I think I must have killed her".

"Oh, Helga you couldn't kill a fly! Shock can do strange things and it has left you with these feelings".

"But what shock, Pat? That's what I want to know! I wish I knew who I was or where I came from, it's an awful thing having to accept the mystery of a lost past".

Patrick held her closer to him then spoke quietly, "Does your head still hurt?".

"Yes - dreadfully!".

He propped himself against the headboard then yanked her between his legs, supporting her back against his body; he proceeded to massage her head with strong but soothing fingers. He massaged the scar that the hair no longer grew on, then used gentle pressure on the crown, firm pressure in between the eye and eyebrow area. He continued across her temples, gradually, soothingly down into her neck. He possessed the powerful and natural healing ability of touch. "Oh Pat, there is such magic in your fingertips", she whispered faintly.

Patrick had learnt the art of self massage to allay his own dreadful headaches that he suffered from occasionally since the case of wine fell on his head. She became very relaxed, her breathing even and eventually fell fast asleep. As he was laying her dead weight into a comfortable position on the bed, part of her body became exposed and revealed the most horrific scarring he had ever seen in his life; he couldn't have imagined worse. They started below her waist and ran down the left buttock. As he stood over her, feeling grief-stricken, the ugly scars became veiled as he looked beyond them to realize the extent of her dreadful suffering. How she had escaped a life threatening infection was beyond comprehension.

He tucked her in gently as if she was the most precious thing in the world then made his way to the bathroom; he sat down on the toilet seat and his body shivered convulsively as he cried like a baby. She had been so badly burnt yet had dragged herself around for God knows how long, only to be chased by the locals.

Should he have to lead a double life he would like nothing more than to protect her from here on in; never let her set foot in Skibbereen again.

He splashed his face with water time and time again, then as he reached for the towel he caught a glimpse of his reflection in the mirror; the face that stared out at him had eyes that were bloodshot and swollen and the memory of his adolescence came back to him. He had been a big lad of seventeen when his mother died; he had gone to the bathroom then to cry but as he stepped out his father threw the hurtful words at him. "Big burly Irishmen don't cry, Patrick, your mother wouldn't have been pleased".

He had never cried from that day to this, never thought he'd need to. "Pardon me, Da", he spluttered, "But even you'd have cried".

With the sound of her light breathing in his ears, memories of the night flooded Patrick's mind and he spontaneously reached out a protective arm to her as he opened his eyes in the darkened room. There was a glimmer of light showing through the edge of the heavily lined green brocade curtains. It wasn't the silver of the moonlight, it was the gold of the sun. He looked at his watch. Damn! They had slept through the whole night, it was now morning. Their intended night of erotic passion hadn't materialised. It was hardly worth the bloody hotel bill especially as they were going to miss their breakfast.

His eyes softened as they fell on her and although he had an immediate erection he knew his love for her went beyond the reverie of physical attraction. He tenderly brushed her hair back from her eyes. Never, in his wildest dreams had he thought himself capable of wanting a woman so much. She stirred and in the darkness turned into his arms - her lips were warm and moist as she sought his; she touched his body and moaned with desire, wanting him badly - couldn't wait. There wasn't going to be time for the preliminaries he fumbled as he prepared himself fast. She moaned again as she drew him into her.

"Oh, my darling...", he murmured as he entered her deeply with the second thrust - then all hell broke loose. There was an anguished screech in his ear, he had never heard a louder scream of terror in his life. "Geoff! Geoff! My Geoff is dead! - Barry! I want Barry!".

"Shhh..! You're alright". He tried to pacify her. She continued to scream frantically. Christ! She'll wake her dead husband!

He jumped out of bed, discarding his protection and pulled his trousers over his naked body. A disturbance started in the hotel corridor, followed by thumping on the bedroom door; he struggled into his shirt while opening it. "It's alright, my lady friend has had a nightmare".

Two female cleaning staff pushed past him. He watched as the two women wrapped a blanket round her. "What happened, my dear?", one of them asked sympathetically, while the other stared accusingly at Patrick. "Did you really have a nightmare or do you wish to make a complaint?"

She was too traumatised to answer, but lifted her head slowly and looked in Patrick's direction. Anything that had been between them had deteriorated rapidly, her eyes were cool and impartial as they met his. He knew she was seeing Patrick, the wine merchant. Pat the wine importer had vanished.

He dragged his eyes from her and said to the women, "Will you see to her? I have a phone call to make".

He picked up the telephone and tapped in the number as if by reflex.

"May I speak to Sir Malcolm's secretary please?".

She watched him with a remote and far-away gaze as he waited to be put through.

"Miss Foster speaking. Can I help you?".

"Patrick O'Rafferty here! I wish to speak to Sir Malcolm without further ado".

It wasn't easy to get past Miss Foster, but there was something very commanding in the Irishman's voice which made her reply, "Putting you through straight away, Mr O'Rafferty".

Sir Malcolm's voice came back agitated and sounding very much like he did not rank Patrick very highly in his esteem, "I do hope this is important, Patrick, as I am a very busy man".

"I reckon, Sir Malcolm, I am about to deliver the most important message of your lifetime. I have unearthed your daughter, alive and well".

It's a long drive and two ferry crossings from the wine regions of Germany. What a hell of a difference five days can make. There were no light thoughts on this journey to occupy his mind as on the outward. Where can one buy cigarettes in this neck-of-the-woods? He had an overbearing need for the weed that he had resisted for three weeks and thought he had quashed the damn habit - he'd stop at the next town, might just blunt the pain.

Teresa had been picked up and whisked away in the private plane from the Braemer's vineyard. Pat and Helga never stayed at the Hotel Krone that night: the Braemer's had fixed it with the hoteliers, who owned vineyards and were friends of theirs. Sure he'd be hailed a hero in Cork, Skibbereen and Bantry on his return for unearthing the beautiful Teresa.

He was humorous and quiet by nature but deep down inside lay an Irish temperament trying to get out as the frenzied roar bounced off the dashboard and blasted the inside of the car, "A hero's welcome I could fuckin' well do without".

Chapter Eight

Jill couldn't bear to face him any longer, she got up and started to pace. The fact that he had been playing one woman off against the other was neither here nor there. It was the cold blooded chicanery and the way they had pulled the wool over everybody's eyes that got to her. What in heaven's name manner of woman was Joanne Debussy to relieve herself of the baby without as much as a glance? What manner of woman had Teresa been to stand there and wait for her lover's baby to come out of another woman's body into her waiting hands? What manner of man had he been for orchestrating it all?

This woman must not take her little girl; she was hers now and nobody was going to take her away from her. She would go to desperate measures to keep the family together.

She stopped pacing for a minute and looked at him; she wished he would stop talking. He had his head in his hands now, muttering on and on and on incoherently about something she didn't want to hear. "Until I met Joanne Debussy music was my escape from reality I was obsessed with it and I cared for virtually nothing else. I always had severe problems with relationships and communicating my inner feelings. Joanne opened a whole new way of life for me and my career took off as she inspired my work by various means; erotic, worldly and domestic. Everything was wonderful for a few years. Gradually, for some reason, she became disenchanted and for three months she wouldn't let me near her".

Jill felt sick. While he was wanting Joanne Debussy he was probably still having it off with Teresa.

"Three months proved long enough to be grief-stricken. I gave up on her, came to terms with it and fell out of love with her. Although I had decided I didn't want to continue working with her, I had to see her just once more to express my sentiments on some lyrics; that was all. When we had dealt with the matter, I held out my hand to her and wished her all the best for the future. I was determined to leave her that night for good. Those three months of rejection led me to believe our goodbye didn't even warrant a kiss. But I was wrong; she threw herself into my arms and begged me to stay for just one more night. I should have left her but...".

Jill glared at him, she finished the sentence in her mind, '... it wasn't only that the flesh was weak, she twisted my arm and, perverse as it may seem, I had to clock off in style'.

His continuing words broke into her inner rage. "In the morning I walked out of there and never looked back. I took the next flight to Cork: there was nowhere in the whole wide world I needed to be more than Skibbereen".

How very, very, nice for Teresa, Jill thought callously, she was the one you really wanted all along.

"You needn't have told me all that Barry, I didn't want to hear it", said Jill in a weary voice.

"I wanted you to know that it is completely over between

Joanne and I. There is nothing between us now and never has been since that night. All the nights I have spent in her company lately have been trying to talk her out of seeing Bonny. I have argued into the early hours, but to no avail. I gave in to her request when she convinced me that she only wanted to see her once; how could I deny a mother that request. When I saw her into the car afterwards, she reneged on her promise and told me she would get her regardless of what means. In light of the new evidence from Sir Malcolm we will have to put up a colossal fight to keep her".

"Up to the present time, she has never once hinted that you were not the father?"

"No!".

"And you have no idea who it could be?".

"Not in my wildest dreams would I ever have imagined her with anyone else".

A sudden realization hit him and he voiced his recollections to Jill. Miki had written the magnificent lyrics for Joanne in the past which won her a Tony Award. He had been married then but was since divorced. It never entered his head at the time, but they did spend a lot of time together working on those lyrics and once, for some reason unknown to him, they had a clash of wills which almost cost her career. Barry assumed it was professional. They reconciled and she later accompanied him to Paris for a performance of the Verdi Requiem. It was indeed possible and very probable, that Miki Delecour was Bonny's father.

Jill knew Miki well, he played with Bonny on the occasions he visited their home.

This was the first day that she and Barry had spent alone together since they moved in. Jane was on a day trip to Cambridge with the Friendship Club and the children were all safely deposited in school. With getting his extravagant new show on the road, among all the other composing obligations, he hadn't time for a day off - he tried to keep weekends free but devoted his time to them all, collectively, as a family. They meticulously planned their week-ends; took jaunts out to the countryside and as they all enjoyed the great outdoors, went on rambles together, enjoying the classic English scenery.

This shattering problem over Bonny had warranted a day off and brought them together.

He stood up. "Jill, there's something else I want to tell you! But before I do, I have a proposition to make to you".

They stood facing each other, grey eyes staring into blue. "I want you to be my wife in every sense of the word".

The significance of his words hit her and she felt weak; she experienced an exulting rush of sexual emotion and her bodily desire for him was such that she would lie down this minute on the goatskin rug upon which they stood or indeed, as they stood - anywhere or any way. She continued to hold his gaze as her body reacted by making her breasts heave and nipples stand firmly against her blouse. The atmosphere was pervaded with an undeniable magnetic union - she wanted to feel the heat of his breath, hear him whisper in her ear, feel his body against her - everything that had happened between them that night so long ago - the phone rang loud! It rang again! A third time! She moved slightly, somebody had to answer it.

Barry restrained her by laying his hand on her shoulder, he was breathless by now, a pulse visibly throbbing in his temple, she could almost hear his heart pound.

"Let it ring! I'm not working today!". The words came in a rasping whisper.

His hand was hot and sweaty as it gripped her shoulder through her flimsy blouse. He wanted her and she was electrified, but she managed to say, "It could be the school, I'd better answer it".

She unlocked their gaze reluctantly and answered the phone.

"Oh, Sir Malcolm, how lovely to hear you".

"Jill, it's imperative that I contact Barry today. Can you give me a number I could reach him on?", his voice was agitated.

Her face fell; something was wrong. She handed Barry the phone and left the room.

Whatever was wrong, she would hear about it soon enough, she needed just a little respite to think; there was a lot on her mind; a lot had been uncovered this morning. The revelations had been a massive turmoil, but things would be alright now that they were going to become willing lovers and everything in their life would be richer without the barriers; making love would be taking communication to the ultimate and no matter how busy his lifestyle or how insurmountable the problems seemed, they would work them out as they held each other in their arms in the night.

A sigh of relief escaped her lips as she sank into one of the plush pale green and cream chairs by the hearth and closed her eyes as she recalled what Barry had told her earlier.

He said that five weeks after their night of passion Joanne rang to tell him she was pregnant. She said she had given it a lot of thought and had made up her mind to have an abortion. He had been shocked and devastated by the news: on one hand, Teresa was pressurising him to have another baby, while on the other, Joanne was contemplating putting his unplanned progeny to death. 'I've got too much on' she had said, '..and anyway I don't want the brat'.

He pleaded with her not to be rash and they arranged to meet.

She wasn't completely heartless and he succeeded in breaking through to her more compassionate nature the appropriate solution of letting Teresa have it, thereby granting the baby life.

He arranged a meeting between them. When Teresa was satisfied that Joanne wouldn't renege at the last minute, she started to circulate the news that she was pregnant again. Teresa and Joanne coincidentally shared the same blood group.

Joanne was able to hide the fact that she was pregnant for four months, then announced she was taking a well earned vacation.

Teresa padded herself as the months went by then she and Geoff took a holiday. Everyone, including Jane, thought they were bonkers to go off so near the time.

The baby was born in Ulster, in the little village of Plumbridge that nestled at the bottom of the Glenelly valley. Geoff, who was completely wrapped around Teresa's little finger, giving in to her every whim, delivered Bonny, with Teresa's help, while Barry paced in the next room.

Teresa and Geoff walked out of there with the baby while Barry stayed with Joanne for four days and during that time, although she was subdued, never once mentioned the little girl she gave birth to. When the time came for them to part, they shook hands; what they should have done on the previous occasion.

Suddenly Barry's excited voice broke into her thoughts. "Jill, you're never going to believe this! It's beyond my wildest dreams and something I could never have anticipated but Patrick came upon Teresa, alive and well, living in a little village in Germany. She had lost her memory but it was rekindled by meeting up with Patrick", he paused only slightly for breath, "Patrick O'Rafferty!", he ejaculated with arms raised in exultation, "I can't wait to shake your hand! Just think, Jill, Teresa might have been lost to us for good if it hadn't been for Patrick".

Jill's face went pale; her mouth trembled as it became parched and she swallowed with difficulty. She felt faint but forced herself to look up at him. Never had she seen such a beaming smile on his face before. If the earlier revelations of the day hadn't stunned her, this certainly did. A woman she had never met had suddenly turned her life upside down and the sharp pain of jealousy felt like a knife being stabbed through her heart, then twisted. In a daze she could hear his voice echoing from the past with an extraordinary vividness *'I am still obsessed and in love with her and will be thinking of her all of my natural life'.* What he had felt for her a short while ago hadn't been the undying love he endured for Teresa, it had simply been unadulterated physical lust. Could there be a more wicked twist of fate at a most inconvenient time?

She got unsteadily to her feet and faced him, willing herself not to cry, she suffered a torment while her entity was threatened; her heart pounded. She was going to miss out in more ways than one now that the woman had returned from the dead. The children - Oh, God, the children! At last she forced herself to speak, albeit selfishly, "Bar-ry, I don't want to lose the children".

His smile died suddenly as if the light had just been switched off and a pitiful expression crept over his face. She could see in his eyes that he knew she was the only liability in this new scenario and he felt sorry for her. "We won't lose the children, Jill, I swear to you". 'We' - he had said - 'we'. "Things will be different, but I'm still their father.   Until we can be assured that Teresa is capable of looking after them, they will remain with us. Sir Malcolm says she is very shook up and will need psychological help before she is in any fit state to look after them.   Hopefully that day will come and when it does, they are still my children and you and I will have access to them whenever we wish. Nobody knows more than me the extent of your love and self-sacrifice towards the children and, Jill, never, ever, underestimate your hold over me".

Despite his protestations she felt devastated. Barry never did have the power of penetrating her mind, but as he said, there was one thing he knew for certain: she loved the children; but they were never a self-sacrifice, more within the context of self-fulfilment. They were her life, the only life she had, or wanted. At the moment he was compassionate towards her, as he was that night when he took advantage of her declaration of love for him and sought solace in her arms simply because of Teresa's death. Next day he rejected her. She wished she could believe him now, but she didn't trust him implicitly, his past record wasn't good. Once he meets up with the one woman in his life who just won't go away, he will scorn her once again or make her suffer in silence in the way Geoff must have done. No, she couldn't delude herself, denying there was a problem, when it would be obvious to everyone else.

The bottom had fallen out of her world. Rejection in favour of another woman was a scenario many woman worried about continually, but the reality of it was insufferable.

Already he had forgotten their animalist state before the phone rang - he would get satisfaction, real satisfaction elsewhere; the *coup de grâce* for their marriage had indeed been swift.

"I'm going to Teresa now! Will you cancel all my appointments for the next three days?".

He proceeded to lay an encouraging hand on her shoulder and she lowered her head as he became sympathetic towards her. "...and don't worry, everything will be alright".

What was the mad rush? Why did he have to leave today - this minute? If he had felt even the slightest spark towards her, he should have stayed with his wife tonight. The other woman, Teresa, wasn't going to disappear again.

She knew in her heart of hearts that he didn't want to hurt her but there was no overall solution that would suit everyone. She would maintain her dignity until he left, but after that, would break down to her heart's content with no stifling of her feelings; then the only honourable thing to do would be to drift off into obscurity, extricate herself completely, granting a clear way for the rest of them to enjoy this miraculous happening.

After he left she slumped pitifully down onto the long haired goatskin rug and cried in devastation, amid shudders, like a demented animal; on this very spot they had stood electrified less than an hour ago and where she would gladly have consummated their love.

Eventually she stood up, red eyed but calm; she had made a new life for herself before and would do it again. Barry Thorpe was diminutive now compared to what she had to do. She picked up the phone and dialled a number. "Michelle, I need help!".

Chapter Nine

Patrick answered the phone - her voice came down the line all sweetness and light.

"Hello, Patrick, and how are you?".

"Hello, Teresa, I'm fine! How are you?".

"Fine, Patrick, fine".

"What can I be doing you for this fine day?".

"Sure have you forgotten about us, Patrick? We're running out of wine".

"What'll you be wanting then? The usual?".

"Well, Barry drops in a lot. Do you know his taste?".

"I know it well. Sure he has the same taste as myself", in more ways than one, "I'll add a case of Halbtrocken".

"When will you have it ready, Patrick?".

"Let's see now; today is the ...".

She cut him short, "Can I have it today, Patrick?".

"I don't see why not. Would this afternoon suit?".

"This afternoon is perfect, just perfect", she said.

"That's fine then, I'll get them to you this afternoon".

"Thank you, Patrick, I'll see you later then".

Patrick replaced the phone. She had a bit of the Irish twang back. He remembered the first time she came about the place. Hoity-toity she was, from the South of England. She adjusted though, and fast. He never knew anyone from those parts to adjust so fast. She had five fluent languages under her belt; was keen to add to that by asking Patrick to teach her some Irish Gaelic. He told her she would have to go to Ballingeary, otherwise up to Donegal, a wee place called Gortahork, for that. She made do by imitating the local accent in Cork and before long it became second nature to her. She was now accepted as a local, which was most unusual for in-comers. But then, as she herself had proved, she could fit in to any area.

Patrick's pencil snapped in his hands under the pressure. He threw it in the waste bin while his thoughts continued. There was a big article in the Cork Examiner covering her reappearance. She told about how she had wandered for days and as the people all spoke German, she thought that she must have been German too. They wanted Patrick to be photographed with her, as the champion, but he refused and made off to France that morning, at short notice.

Business was a bit slack at the moment, he could do with a few more orders, although secure enough, it wasn't exactly booming. He called to John who was loading up his van, "John, will you make up Mrs Webb's usual order

of wine, plus a case of Braemer's Halbtrocken and deliver
it this afternoon".

"Sure, Patrick, sure. But don't you ... ?".

Patrick interrupted, "No, John! I'm far too busy".

John pulled the van up outside the front door of
'Checkerberry'. It was a massive place this and he
wondered if he should have gone round the back; Patrick
always made a point of delivering this order himself, even
before Michelle ever came about the place. He opened
the van door, got out and stood gazing about him, then he
saw the figure of Mrs Webb in the distance across the
gardens; it seemed as if she was gathering flowers. She
looked in his direction and started to run, then gradually
slowed down until eventually a walking pace.

"Good afternoon, John", she called as she approached,
waving a little bunch of herbs. "It's yourself then?".

"Good afternoon, Mrs Webb. Yes, it's myself, Patrick's
busy".

"Awful busy is he?".

"Yes, awful busy", he answered.

John opened the back of the van and removed a case of
wine. Teresa picked up the case beneath it, saying, "I'll
show you where it goes, John, follow me".

John was astounded and went hastily after her, yelling, "Mrs Webb, for crying our loud! Put that wine down! Sure no woman would be expected or able to carry that weight".

She looked round with twinkling eyes and laughed at him, "This woman was expected to do it, John, and this woman was able".

She carried in half the wine with the ease of any man, locked his van and handed him the key. "That's it all in now, John, and thank Patrick for me".

She watched and waved as he drove off then walked slowly into the house. It was quiet; she was on her own for the first time since she came back. The children and Jane were in London visiting her parents.

The time dragged till 7.0'Clock when she knew he would be home from the warehouse, then she picked up the phone and dialled.

"Hello, Patrick, this is Teresa again".

"Hello, Teresa", said Patrick, sounding surprised. "You got your wine alright?".

"Yes thanks, Patrick, but John forgot to bring the Halbtrocken that I wanted for Barry. I'm very disappointed, Patrick. You see, I'm expecting him tonight".

"I could have sworn I saw him loading it in the van.

Don't worry Teresa, I always keep some here in the house, I'll take you over a case out of my own stock. Bejabbers, Teresa hold on ... !".

He ran to the kitchen and pulled the charred steak from under the grill. "Damn! Damn!", he roared and made his way back to the phone.

"I've burnt my steak to a cinder. I'll have to do another one, so I'll not be over till 8.30".

"I caused you to burn your steak, Patrick, so don't do another one. I'll have one for you when you come".

"No, Teresa! No!", said Patrick urgently, but the line went dead.

Even though Patrick had taken extra trouble with his appearance; showered, shaved and adorned his best shirt and tie, he still felt he should dump the wine outside her door and scarper. He hadn't set eyes on her since then; hadn't wanted to.

No such luck, she was waiting for him, so no chance of him getting the hell out. He felt very uptight as he got out of the car.

"Hello, Teresa". He noticed her pallor.

"Hello, Patrick". She noticed him tense.

She held out her hand to him. The handshake was familiar as they clasped hands in a tight grip but she was

Teresa and he was Patrick. Seeing her for the first time in six months in the flesh, not as a dream, shook him to the core. She was beautiful, so very beautiful, but this lady was unapproachable; elegant and chic, immaculately dressed to the nines in silk; way - way out of his class.

The table was set for two and the aroma was appealing.

"When are you expecting Barry?", he asked, trying to sound indifferent.

"He's just rang; he can't make it tonight. Will you put a bottle of that half-dry in the fridge to chill? I'll be straight back".

Taking his time, after extracting one bottle, he picked up the case of wine and trod the well known route to the cellar. He made his way back to the fridge, opened it and read the label of the Halbtrocken half-dry with wandering attention. He was about to deposit it in a space when an unaffected and well loved voice reached his ears: "Pat O'Rafferty, can we continue where we left off?".

He froze where he stood, then slowly, very slowly placed the bottle in the fridge, pressed it shut and turned. She had her hair tied back in a pony tail lending to a little girl look and was wearing a floral dress with a scooped neckline that fell over her striking figure exquisitely; around her wrist a silver charm bracelet; her eyes alive and flirtatious, with a glisten of a tear ready to spill out. This girl was delectable and delightfully approachable; he held out his arms to her. Her tear spilled over as she raised her face to him and went into his outstretched arms.

"Oh, Pat O'Rafferty, Pat O'Rafferty, you would never guess just how very much I've missed that unaffected personal Irish charm".

He felt completely rejuvenated as he held her ever so tight pressing his lips on hers, quietening her; the fact that she was the type of woman that needed two men and that this could be a clandestine affair didn't bother him; he was only too glad to be one side of the triangle. "My God, how I have missed you! It was beyond my wildest dreams that I would ever hold you again".

"It wasn't beyond my dreams, Pat, we were destined for each other and I have thought of you every day since I came back".

"Are you happy to be home, my darling? It's six months now, isn't it?".

"I'm happy now that I've got you, but I'd be happier still if I had my little girl back".

Patrick was saddened by her words and held her closer to him in consolation, before saying, "If anyone is well looked after its Bonny, please believe me!".

"Yes, yes. Everyone tells me that! I've got to believe it".

Then in a playful mood and with her head to one side, Teresa said, "Well, are we going to start at exactly where we left off, Pat".

"I don't know how to start on the third thrust, but I'll make a damn good stab at it". He beamed happily as he swept her up into his arms. "Let me see if I can find your bedroom in this massive house".

Chapter Ten

Jill sat in the car strumming her fingers on the steering wheel. He said he would be here around 9.O'Clock, it was now twenty minutes past. She was slightly anxious but he had been late before, she would wait for as long as it took, he was reliable and would come eventually.

It was seven months since Jill walked out that night and left the boys in Jane's care. It had been heartbreaking and the thought of it now brought tears to her eyes as they had done on many, many occasions. She felt justified in taking Bonny with her, after all she was legally her mother, as she was the boys. The papers had just been signed before Teresa turned up. There was no way she would hand Bonny over to her natural mother, she would die first.

After she rang Michelle, everything had to go on as normal till the time was right for her to leave. Every second of that day would live in her memory for ever.

Jill had driven to the school, parked the car and went into the kindergarten. She noticed Bonny straight away and went to her. Bonny held out her arms. Miss Segal came up to Jill, saying, "She has been a little off colour today Mrs Thorpe, but didn't want to miss the singing, so I decided I would keep my eye on her rather than ask you to collect her earlier. I hope you don't mind. Even though she wasn't well, she still sang better than the others".

"You did right, Miss Segal. If she hasn't improved by tomorrow, I'll keep her home".

As they waited in the car Jill was anxious and checked her temperature with the back of her hand. Bonny opened her mouth and asked her to have a look at her cough; she smiled and had a peep at her tonsils. Shortly, Iain came running, followed closely by Alan. Their eyes always lit up when they saw her and she felt broken hearted that day. She didn't usually kiss them in greeting, they thought it was soft, didn't want their friends to see. That day was different, she kissed them.

Iain spoke excitedly, "Jill, Alan is in my class now for maths, he's caught up".

"Good for you, Alan! I'm really pleased". Alan raised his eyebrows and with a gleam in his eye displayed a confident smug smile.

In a few minutes Jamie came charging at the double, "Jill, guess what? Mr Connelly would like you and I to do a duet on the flute next Wednesday. Oh Jill, you will come, won't you?".

She kissed him and held him to her for a second, "I'd love to Jamie"- It was Friday; next Wednesday was a million years away.

She drove in the direction of the Railway Station to pick up Jane. Bonny, although not well, was talking excitedly about going on the train.

"We're not going on the train, Bonny", said Jamie.

"Yes, we are", said Bonny.

"No, we are not, we are collecting Jane from the Station", said Jamie knowingly.

"We are going on the train! We are! We are!", said Bonny and started to hit Jamie.

Jamie hit her back and pulled her hair. Bonny screamed. Jill pulled in. They continued to fight. She dropped her head on the steering wheel; it wasn't the fact they were fighting that got to her, it was simply that she was going to miss all this healthy bickering.

Jane arrived, spent a few minutes biding her friends goodbye, then got into the car. She would have observed straight away that something was bothering Jill as she spoke about her day in Cambridge. "Oh, the bikes! I spent my day dodging bikes. Hundreds of students on bikes coming at you from all directions. Bonny, you would have loved the Teddy Bear shop - and Jill, you look as if you could do with a treat, well I've got the very thing - the most delicious Chelsea buns from Fitzbillies".

In the dead of night Jane and Michelle put the sleeping and still ailing child in the car, while Jill took a last look at Iain, Alan and Jamie. Her two good women friends assisted and stood by her that night for what they believed to be right.

In the early days Jill's imagination ran away with her. She suffered a torment as she pictured Teresa being pampered by everyone. There would be a little vase of herbs on her breakfast tray, she would relish in the mixed aromas as she poured the milk and sugar on her corn flakes while the children crawled all over the bed in a state of euphoria. It wasn't long till the sad news reached her; she couldn't have been more wrong. The children were hostile and indifferent after the first initial excitement and wanted Barry to take them home. Jamie had said Jill would be worried about them and they had to practice some tunes for Wednesday.

The tears ran from Jill's eyes as she rested her head on the steering wheel. She dabbed them then checked her watch again. He was forty minutes late. She pressed the lever and moved the seat into a reclining position to get more comfortable. Her thoughts continued: The news had reached her that Teresa had became badly affected by it all and tried to cover her feelings of regret and dismay as best she could. Barry had assured her it was a natural reaction as Jill had gone out of her way to become a loving mother to them.

Teresa had also became phobic about looking at Bonny's pictures, she thought she had killed her. Everyone around convinced her that Bonny was alive and well and would be safe with Jill who loved her. She was completely aware and annoyed at the irrationality of her reaction but was unable to overcome it; it was a source of great discomfort, terror, humiliation and embarrassment. A psychologist put her through a type of therapy to rid her of her phobia. The new treatment had a subtle approach whereby the sufferer is exposed to the phobic situation for as long as they can tolerate the fear until the point where they no longer feel the anxiety.

He was an hour late and it was getting cold. She turned

on the engine and let it idle; it would take ages before it generated any heat and she wished that she had brought a rug.

Yes, she heard it all! Thank god she had been able to get in touch with the children, albeit under wraps. She had been able to communicate and instil in them the necessity of accepting their mother, who, through no fault of her own, was going through enormous regressional anxieties. Teresa went out of her way and with the cooperation of the children she succeeded in the mammoth task of winning back their love, at last.

It was chilly outside and with the engine running the windows of the car became steamed up with her breath. Wiping a patch she looked through and saw a car pulling up in front of hers at last. Thank God. The outline of the approaching figure in the darkness set her heart thumping at full bat, her throat asphyxiating instantly as she realized who it was. She opened her mouth to scream but no sound came.

Chapter Eleven

"Shit!", breathed Patrick, as the Captain announced they were being diverted to Schipol Airport in Amsterdam due to trouble in one engine. It was now 6 O'Clock and this delay was going to knock his schedule haywire.

The passengers were all agitated, some more and others to a lesser degree than Patrick. They had been told the delay would be for at least an hour and to await an announcement regarding their re-scheduled departure time.

They entered the ground floor of the main oblong arrivals/departure lounge at Schipol. He sauntered slowly around; there was a good selection of shops so Patrick tried to push in time wandering through them, one after the other; camera and radio, glassware, leather. There was a Dutch food shop, some of the women folk made a bee-line for that. He went up to the next floor; diamonds and gems, he'd give that a by, there was no way he could ever afford her category of taste. She would be able to buy those things for herself, without doubt she was being sustained by Sir and Dr. The Executive Lounge was on this level but being an ordinary sort of bloke, he wasn't a member, didn't want to be.

He made his way to the ground floor again and went into the International lounge where he ordered himself a double whisky and soda before taking a corner seat in the smoker's area. He lit up and straight away thought of the women in his life who depended on him; he only wanted one! God, how he loved every inch of her scarred body.

She had been astounded at his acceptance of her ugly scars and eventually spoke to him of how she awakened to the intolerable and excruciating pain, not knowing what had happened to her.

"The pain was so dreadful that my consciousness slowly left me and I experienced a marvellous feeling that I was making an exquisite escape from it as I glided in a languid and buoyant state with a renewed stamina over the charred physical body lying under the vines which I seemed to be disassociated with. I felt as if I was in a vivid, bright and happy state and drifted over the fields and treetops tall looking down on the winding river; then I had a wild urge to return. I became worried in case I had drifted too far and would never find my way back. When I eventually found the vines again, I saw the body and it seemed rested and refreshed so I returned into it.

"I know these were hallucinations and wishful self-delusions but they allowed me to survive as I thought I was functioning independently of the charred body. With mind over matter, a force unleashed the body's remarkable regenerative forces and the pain steadily decreased until it eventually disappeared".

Patrick knew she would have died if she hadn't created her own highly persuasive philosophy of healing, thereby influencing the body's natural healing mechanisms.

As he thought of her now his body reacted to his need of her and he tossed back a large mouthful of whisky as he tried to allay his hunger for her.

An adverse streak had entered the arena; he wanted more than her body. It was like crying for the moon - he winced slightly - if he wasn't careful being fetish would ruin everything else that was beautiful between them.

The ash dropped from his unsmoked cigarette onto the table - it disintegrated as he polluted the air by blowing it with a macho force.

An announcement came over the loudspeaker with information for his flight number, he listened intently. Damn! Their plane was grounded indefinitely. All passengers would be accommodated on the next plane due in from Cologne, forty five minutes after touch-down. He looked up towards the monitor. The next plane due in was from Lyon in ten minutes, Cologne, thirty minutes later. He swilled the last of his drink and decided he would stretch his legs for a while and - make a phone call.

"Oh, darling, you woke me up. I had one of those damned headaches so retired early".

"Darling, I'm sorry, I just had to hear your voice again".

"I'm glad you woke me, Pat. I love you so very much!".

"I love you too, darling, I can't wait to hold you".

"I can't wait to have you inside me. I wish you had left it behind when you went away".

"You mean like a ...".

"Yes, just like that". They both laughed.

"I'll let you get back to sleep again so I'll say goodbye now, darling. I just wanted to hear your voice".

"Bye, darling, have a nice trip".

"Are you still there, darling?", said Patrick

"Yes, I'm still here. I love you, darling".

"I wish I was there to massage your headache away".

"I know you do, darling. Your fingers are magic. For all we know, you might have massaged my memory back that night".

"Your memory certainly came back with a vengeance. My love for Helga was suddenly superseded by my love for Teresa". He hesitated, "Try and get back to sleep again, darling, sorry I woke you. Bye, darling. Sleep well".

"Oh, darling! don't forget to tell Karl Heinz and Frau Braemer, Franz and Rudolf...".

"I'd never forget that, sweetheart, they miss you so much".

"Tell them...".

"I'll tell them, I love you. Goodnight, darling".

"Bye, darling".

"Are you still there...?".

As Patrick replaced the phone the Lyon flight passengers were filing into the foyer and straight away the figure of Barry Thorpe caught his eye. He gave him an icy stare as he watched him stop to sign an autograph for a woman; another woman strung on behind her, then a man. The damned man was always treated with elaborate courtesy by everyone, while his every move was watched. He never liked the cursed philanderer since he heard the children were his; he could have sworn Geoff and he were best friends. In Patrick's estimation, the worst thing a man can do is bang his best friend's wife. We're not friends, let alone good friends, but I wonder what he would think and do if he knew I was banging his woman on a Monday, Wednesday and Friday for the past month?

Patrick scrutinized him; the bugger was damned attractive, not one congenital deficiency in sight and he exuded power and class which would present itself as an aphrodisiac to women. Now that they were sharing Teresa he noticed everything about him, strange how it seemed to go over his head previously. It irritated Patrick as he realized the man wasn't even aware of his appealing looks.

Still, he had his cross to bear with all the unwelcome publicity. Dammit! What the hell! He'd join the queue! Might as well exchange a few pleasantries with the cursed man, it would pass a bit of time if nothing else.

Barry was getting agitated when he realized there was a queue forming. As he signed for the man in front of Patrick, he lifted his head and said, "Sorry I'm ... Patrick! My God, Patrick O'Rafferty! This is a pleasant surprise. Are you staying in Amsterdam?".

Barry smiled broadly while Patrick smiled faintly as they shook hands.

"No, I'm grounded here, worse luck", he replied.

Barry took command, saying, "I would invite you to the Executive Lounge but by the sound of it you need a break from here; we will go over to the Hilton Hotel, its no distance. I would welcome a word with you, Patrick, I should have contacted you sooner".

Patrick nodded his agreement and followed.

They ordered drinks in the Schipol Hilton lounge and moved over to an area which was slightly less conspicuous.

Their conversation was nothing more than desultory. "How is Michelle, Patrick, I haven't seen her for ages?".

"Oh, fine. Just fine".

"No wedding bells in the offing?".

"No! She's a loyal and dedicated dame you know, tied up

with the McGurkins". Then Patrick ventured shrewdly with caution, "What about Jill? Heard anything?".

Barry didn't answer him with words, he reacted to the question by nodding no and lowering his eyes. Then compelling himself to be more cheerful he said, "Patrick, I never did thank you for unearthing Teresa. I will be forever indebted to you".

Patrick threw a mouthful of whisky into the back of his throat. Yes, he thought, I helped you lose a wife so that you could reinstate your mistress. As for myself, I've gained a mistress and lost my goal and stimulus for the future. His need of her was tremendous but the hole-in-the-corner affair had lost its appeal, it was crumbling in on him, he wanted the woman body and soul. He had stopped wanting to share her but had insufficient capital to propose to her.

How could he expect her to keep within the slender confines of his limited means? He hadn't a ghost of a chance compared to this man who had so much more to offer. There was no question of her ever being asked to choose between them, he hadn't the right. He suddenly felt like scum in the eyes of the musician, who was in this very position some time ago, playing second-fiddle in her affections.

Barry was speaking between gulps of whisky. She had the same effect on them both, thought Patrick, as he watched him and listened lethargically. He was talking of things Patrick already knew about. Her problems of adjustment; her phobias, terrors and anxieties and how she eventually mastered all. Then the concluding words came through Barry's lips that hit him like a thunderbolt, "It was remarkable that the only disfigurement on her body was the scar on the back of her head, which is unnoticeable with her hair tied back".

Patrick's voice could only reach a whisper as he repeated the word, "Remarkable!".

Why, the damned man had her every Saturday and Sunday! Had he not managed to get the slip off yet? Did he never run his hands underneath it?

There was a prolonged silence then Barry spoke with intense concentration. "Its wonderful having Teresa back, but I'm not a happy man, Patrick, not by a long shot".

Patrick, who was still staggered by the earlier revelation, looked at him intensely. This man, who seemingly had it all, had gloom and doom written all over his face; he was no longer hiding behind a charade.

Barry, meeting Patrick's gaze, said, "Teresa and I are not, and never have been, lovers".

The words bombarded Patrick's ears and he quickly checked his wrist watch. Christ! He was going to miss his plane, but what the hell, this could be worth waiting to hear.

Chapter Twelve

Eamon McGurkin, a Commercial Manager of an Irish Milk Co-operative, caught the flight from Schipol airport to Cork. He wondered where Patrick had taken himself off to. They had called his name over the loudspeaker output system twice to proceed to gate ten for the flight to Cologne. He had met him a few times when he called for Michelle. A nice bloke, too damned nice to be strung along.

Eamon was returning from three days of negotiating a joint venture deal concerned with a milk Co-operative at Veghel, eighty kilometres south east of Schipol. He was mentally drained as the Dutch were tough negotiators but was exceedingly pleased with the outcome of his visit.

It was nine months now since Nona had died. She had been aware of a heart murmur since she was a teenager and, although not thought to be serious, had to take things easy and opt out of sport at school. Eamon had gone along to the Consultant Physician to find out more about it before starting a family. The technical details meant little to him - the tricuspid diastolic flow murmur had originated from an intraventricular septal defect - it was the warning that there could be a problem in pregnancy that worried him and he tried to convince Nona that he could happily resign himself to not having a family; they had each other and that was all that mattered to him. She was, however, on a different wavelength and was determined to take the risk. The Lord was good to them, she came through with flying colours and gave birth to Rory.

Eighteen happy months later she started to become broody again. Eamon knew that in the circumstances it was inadvisable and didn't want another child and blamed himself for her death; he should have imposed his will on her not to tempt fate once again. The baby was kept in hospital until after the funeral; ironically the most traumatic part had been collecting Becky from the hospital that day, he was in the depths of despair as the love he felt for the child was practically nil, he couldn't bring himself to kiss his newborn child. His mother moved in but it soon became apparent that she wasn't going to be able to cope. Rory was too high spirited and the baby was irritable and cross.

Eamon led a busy life so left the selection of a nanny to his mother; the only stipulation he had given her was that she would preferably be a woman in her forties with experience behind her and love children above anything else. When he first met the nanny he was disappointed and wondered what the others were like if she was the best of the bunch. He treated the girl with scepticism; she looked too young, too good looking, fair of skin, and probably had her head full of that boy-friend of hers that she never stopped talking about.

First impressions couldn't have been more wrong and she proved herself to be a very capable and dedicated young lady. Becky lost her irritability and became placid and content in the gentle and loving arms of Michelle and it seemed no time at all before he was confident enough to leave his children entirely in her accomplished hands. Before long she was running the house competently, single handed, he hadn't meant it to be that way but she wouldn't hear of him taking on a housekeeper when his mother reverted to her old lifestyle and moved back into her own home. It was only under duress that she accepted a raise in salary. She was skilful to the point of being extraordinary and in no time at all earned Rory's affections and respect by using a technique that allowed him flexibility without having to set rigorous standards.

She sensed the situation between Becky and himself but made no reference to it; organized group activities whereby Eamon was no longer able to ignore his baby daughter. While Michelle busied herself with Rory, one way or another, Eamon was very often left holding the baby. It was beyond his comprehension now as to how he could ever have frozen that delightful baby out of his love.

A gradual attraction developed between Eamon and Michelle which they were unable to resist.

He remembered the first night well that it came to a head. Together they bathed and played with the children, then when they were tucked in at last, the ambience between them was electric. He had said to her tenderly, "You know what is happening, don't you? I believe I am falling in love with you".

She met his steady gaze and replied simply, "Me too".

Their lips met in a kiss as soft as the Irish mist and from then on she seemed to blossom from a fresh young bud into a passionate flower in full bloom.

As the plane came in to land at Cork airport his thoughts were charging ahead. Three days and three nights apart from her and his children was absolute hell. He visualized her waiting for him - she would join him to look at his sleeping children then they would retreat to bed where they would succumb to a predominant and blissful need for each other.

His mother was forever speculating as to whom he should marry; she knew of quite a few ladies suitable to become the next Mrs McGurkin. He would have to bring things to a head very soon and get it all out in the open. His main worry was that she, in her loyalty, would reject him in favour of Patrick O'Rafferty.

A thought went through his mind again 'I wonder where Patrick took himself off to?'.

Chapter Thirteen

The two men faced each other across the table while Barry bared his soul. "Geoff and Teresa were a desperate couple and spent time and money on useless infertility treatment at a renowned London Hospital. However, they discovered that the fault lay with Geoff and put him on a masculinizing hormone, an androgen. Although it had a fair success with other sub-fertile men, it had no effect on Geoff. They both went through years of torment before deciding to take me into their confidence. They were so desperate I gave in to their request that I should be the donor of the sperm; in a way it was emotional blackmail, but I loved them both. I agreed to the absolute secrecy between the three of us and that there should be nothing in writing that would jeopardise Geoff's complete parentage of the child and to guarantee no heartache in future years. Geoff carried out the artificial insemination to the medical rules at his own clinic. I arrived by private plane at the critical time, after thorough temperature taking ensured ovulation. We all went through an emotional upset when nothing happened first time and had to go through it all again and wept with joy when we discovered that it had worked and that Teresa was pregnant.

"It was rewarding in more ways than one - after the pregnancy was confirmed; Geoff and Teresa were joyously in love again and regained their tremendous sex life which had gone through difficulties because of the infertility".

Patrick lowered his head. He felt no jealousy, just mortification for encroaching into Teresa's private sex life with Geoff.

Barry continued to speak. "I purposely kept away from the twins until they were three months old, and until the day Geoff and Teresa's plane crashed, I felt no paternal feelings towards them other than being plain Uncle Barry. They made marvellous parents and when they wanted to increase their family, I obliged again. Then with Bonny, well - ".

Patrick watched Barry in his hesitant struggle for words, then relieved the awkward predicament by speaking. "You obviously confided all of this to Jill?".

"No! I was about to tell her but the miraculous news of Teresa's return shrouded everything else that day and I couldn't wait to be with her".

Patrick felt sorry for the man whose eyes seldom lit with laughter and who seemed to be in a continual state of worried tension. He needed to ask one question, it was of the utmost importance. "Do you love Jill?".

"Yes, I love her more than anything or anybody in the world, but she doesn't love me. She loved me once, of that I am certain, but I thought I wasn't worthy of her so I made it my business to quash that love she felt for me and without doubt I succeeded. I only hope she is happy now wherever she is and that she has built a good life for herself and Bonny. I don't doubt that if I set the police on her trail I might unearth her, but for what? Once the law got in on it they would cause all sorts of problems, maybe even take Bonny from her. I ruined her life once, I have no intention of doing that to her again".

Patrick quietly deliberated to himself, but only for a minute. "I know where Jill is, I am meeting her tonight". He looked at his watch, "There is no way I can get there on time".

"Christ Almighty! How long have you known?". Barry nearly blew his top.

"Calm down man! Somebody had to help her! Her world was disintegrating around her. Bonny wasn't Teresa's, nor was she yours, she decided if anybody was going to have her, it should be her rather than the other woman. I placed them with a very good friend of mine in the Mosel".

Barry's voice seemed to change pitch and intonation as he spoke recklessly. "So you know all the sordid details regarding Bonny as well then. Just how close are you and she? How is Mrs Thorpe, as she still is, paying you for abetting her? She hasn't touched one penny of my money therefore she has nothing to offer, well, except perhaps her body; does she open up her legs for y... ?".

Patrick reached across the table, the near empty glass crashed to the floor as he picked him up by the scruff of the neck. "No Barry, she does not!", he screeched through clenched teeth.

"Dr Thorpe, would you like me to throw this maniac out?", said a uniformed official rushing to Barry's rescue.

Patrick let go his hold of him; the two men glared at each other.

"No! No! I reckon I'm the most uncouth maniac this decent man has ever had in his company", said Barry straightening his tie and dismissing the defender with a wave of his hand. The uniformed man looked quizzically from one man to the other before moving off.

"Please accept my apology, Patrick, it was the coarse side of me rearing its ugly head. It was an entirely unwarranted and gratuitously offensive thing to say".

Patrick unyieldingly refused to voice his acknowledgement of the apology for the filthy insult. Barry, without the feedback, waited until he observed him relaxing into his seat thereby assuring him of his acceptance before speaking further.

"I want to meet her, Patrick! For Christ sake let me meet her!".

"I'd be breaking a promise, Barry, she trusts me".

"For Christ sake I've told you I love the woman. I'm not exactly going to do her any harm. Just for a moment put yourself in my position, Patrick, if it was Michelle that had absconded and I was concealing her, wouldn't you do anything to get to her?".

Patrick didn't think it was a good similarity, lovely as Michelle was, in his present dilemma he could see her far enough. Now, Teresa - that was different.

"You will have to get the next flight to Cologne. I was to meet her at 9.O'clock, but she makes allowances for flight delays and if I know her, she will wait all night if need be. I never meet up with her where I placed her but if there is any problem, here is Frau Wedikind's address".

There were two flights out to Cork tonight, Patrick would just make the second; the urgency to be in the Mosel had gone; he would postpone his business arrangements until next week, he badly needed to be with Teresa now that he was assured of the entirety of her love.

Schipol airport was not a place he frequented, he had changed planes at it a few times on his way to somewhere else. It was one of those airports that a third of the passengers, at any one time, are just passing through. He had an hour to push in before his flight would be called; the damn place would be imprinted on his mind for ever and he felt he could make his way to the bar under blindfold.

He settled down in the same smoker's area with another whisky and soda in front of him. This would definitely have to be his last alcoholic drink of the evening otherwise he would need to leave his car at Cork airport and call a taxi. He would take it easy: one whisky, one cigarette in one hour.

He thought of Jill and the many encounters they had over the past months, mostly business-like. His first reaction had been one of consternation when Michelle asked him if he would take a few passengers with him, seeing he was going anyway. Bloody women and their problems; he liked the girl well enough, but why him? Look where it had landed him before. At the end of the day, it might have been better if he had left Helga to fate and hadn't bothered his arse with the costly plonk that never sold either; sure half the country had no taste for fine wine - stout was more their line.

On the way to Germany, that first day, everything went smoothly; Bonny asked no questions when Jill told her she would have to stay with him for the ferry crossing. All of the Webb children loved and trusted him as if he was a member of the family. Once they were on the boat he took her to the children's play area and they merged inconspicuously with the other fathers and children. She didn't want to play for long as she was slightly off colour, so she climbed on his knee and fell asleep for the rest of the voyage.

Frau Wedikind thought the world of Patrick, they had the same capacity for fun and mischief and it was for his sake she concealed Jill and Bonny. He knew that he had her wrapped around his little finger and when he approached her, she said, 'Patrick, if you want this woman and her child protecting, then she must need it'.

Before long a close bond developed between the two women. For the first four months, although Jill had been mentally bruised, she was neither positively happy or actively unhappy. She kept a low profile and enjoyed her new interests; teaching a variety of subjects to an exclusive clientele arranged by Frau Wedikind. Having no text books she made up her own training material presenting ideas and concepts in a clear and concise way, her intellect shining through. The feedback Frau Wedikind got from the students was marvellous: They felt that a lot of the success of her training activity lay with the great chemistry that seemed to develop between them; even the most creative training material would be ineffective without it.

Gradually Jill became worried about being too indulgent with Bonny, also there was the matter of her constricted existence. Eventually it all turned sour and she started to fret when realizing how futile it all was. While Bonny was getting plenty of encouragement from Jill to sing, she really needed to develop her talent with proper lessons and training.

The exchange of the letters between the children wasn't an ideal solution but at least communication was maintained, giving hope and light at the end of the tunnel. Jill usually came to meet Patrick on her own, but there were occasions when he visited Frau Wedikind and had a chance of seeing Bonny. It was obvious to him that she missed her brothers and was beginning to wonder when she would see them again; she savoured each sentence of the hand written notes from each of them as one would greet a burst of sunshine on a dull day.

Patrick smiled as he remembered the day he snatched a few hours off his tasting regime and took both Bonny and Jill to the woods to see the grey squirrels defying gravity as they leapt from branch to branch, then on to the next tree. It seemed to lift Jill temporarily and she was as invigorated as the child, thoroughly enjoying herself. She charged through the woods ahead of him calling, "Patrick, hurry yourself. Why are you such a slowcoach?".

He hadn't felt like dashing through the woods as they seemed to want to do; he wanted to enjoy the fresh air and rambling colourful wild flowers. It was the essence of his Irish temperament to take life at a stroll.

He eyed her from behind as a man invariably eyes up a good looking woman with arresting beauty; she had a great figure, her legs bare, slender but strong, smooth and golden. The musician must have lost his marbles to let her walk out of his life without lifting a finger to find her. Didn't he miss those strong legs gripping him tightly as they made love? Christ! Why the hell would he? Didn't he have Teresa! He felt like sending a Tarzan bull-ape roar echoing from one end of the woods to the other when he suddenly saw her turn and smile back, urging him on, then trip over an exposed tree root that was hidden by great clumps of weeds and fall headlong into a mass of rotten, soggy leaves.

He rushed to help her up. "I can't get up, Patrick, I think I've done my ankle in".

He teased her humorously as he manoeuvred her to a moss covered area, propped her against a tree trunk and felt around the joint of her ankle knowledgeably. "No broken bones. You'll have to stay there - you needn't think I'm going to carry a heavy weight like you". He stepped over her and followed Bonny.

His mood lightened as he said to Bonny, "We'll just leave

Jill there, maybe some knight in shinin' armour will ride by and rescue her".

Jill watched helplessly as he and Bonny blithely chased after anything that moved, disrupting the small animal's peaceful habitat. Long-tailed tits flapped through the dwarf shrubs in alarm; rabbits scampered around their feet but were too fast for them. Eventually he caught a baby squirrel and handed it to the excited Bonny. It squealed as she gripped it too tight.

"Please let me keep it, Patrick. I can play with it just like I used to play with Milly".

He persuaded her that if it didn't die before they got the length of the car it certainly would within a few days as it would miss its mummy. She ever so sullenly let it go free.

Jill winced with pain as he once again inspected her slightly swollen ankle but became amused when he said, "I'll come back for you the day after tomorrow, maybe by that time you will have shed some of that weight".

He eventually slung her over his shoulder; she was a ton weight and he wished she hadn't charged so deep into the woods. Alas, he was no Tarzan and almost collapsed with exhaustion as he made his way through the tangled mass of trees and shrubs. When he got to within ten feet of the car he set her down unable to manage another step. As soon as her feet touched the ground, she gave her ankle a jerk and said, giggling, "Oh, look Patrick, I can walk - it's alright now".

Patrick was completely winded and bent over to get his breath back. "Jill Thorpe", he gasped with difficulty, "One way or another, you will pay for this".

Almost two months went by before he saw her again; that was six weeks ago now.

He checked the clock, the flight should be called in fifteen minutes. His thoughts went back to Barry's coarse insinuation and the words he had uttered afterwards 'I reckon I'm the most uncouth maniac this decent man has ever had in his company'. He quickly drained the last of his whisky and wished he could order another. He lit up another cigarette; Christ! he was chain smoking.

She was on a particularly low ebb that night, as was he. The fun and games in the woods were forgotten and she seemed to have sunk to a new low.

It had been very difficult for them both over those last months, believing that the partners they loved had rekindled their passionate affair. Jill didn't know of his longing for Teresa but she knew all was not well between him and Michelle and his warmth and ready humour was waning. She was pale and subdued that evening as she handed over the letters for the boys and deposited the return mail in her handbag.

"I wish I knew what to do, Patrick; it's becoming more and more of a worry; we are existing but it is all so hopeless and I'm running out of the capacity to keep going". A heavy sigh escaped her lips.

He knew she appreciated the times they could be together; he offered her the crucial emotional support she badly needed and kept her just below the threshold of breakdown. Ah! He remembered something; reaching into the glovebox of his car, he drew out a half bottle of brandy and unscrewed the top. "Medicinal purposes! Here, take a slug, you're a bigger bundle of nerves than usual tonight". She hesitated only for a second then reached for the bottle and very cautiously and lady-like let it trickle into her mouth in minuscule drops. They conversed quietly; he conveyed all the news from home that hadn't been communicated through the usual channels and she in turn unloaded her concerns.

He put a cigarette between his lips and was searching for matches in his pocket when he saw she was still taking the occasional sip of the brandy. Pulling the cigarette out of his mouth he said, "Hey! Jesus, Jill, don't drink any more of that brandy or you'll be pissed out of your mind!". He yanked the bottle from her, screwed on the top then held it up to check the quantity. She had taken the equivalent of a double - should do her more good than harm.

He felt pity coupled with a warming of his heart towards her as he lit up his cigarette then wound down the window. Her eyes had brightened slightly, had less of a disheartened look about them and the frown had disappeared from her brow. Her skin was as always translucent and clear, but with an extra flush due to the brandy. If it hadn't been for the reek of booze and smoke, the car would have been full of her niceness; she always smelt nice, sweetly nice; a light and fresh fragrance, honeysuckle talc rather than a heavy exotic perfume.

His eyes ventured over the contours of her body and he observed how her clothes were always fresh and crisp; he noted her clean unpolished fingernails as she nervously fingered her blouse buttons. She was the type of woman who would probably wear snow white underwear rinsed in a fabric conditioner, her rounded breasts bra-less against the soft cotton; they would feel supple, warm and smooth to the touch. His eyes strayed to her slim and flat abdomen and wondered what it would be like to plunge himself deep into her receptive body. He became highly aroused; Christ! She was the last person he would have expected to give him a hard on but she was a sexually repressed woman and he wouldn't say no to a chance of satisfying her womanly needs. He dragged his eyes upwards and looked at her luscious lips, they were naturally pink and full as they quivered slightly making a slow and deliberate effort to speak. "Patrick, you wouldn't take it the wrong way if I were to ask you to put your arm around me?".

He ventured to put a genial arm around her and she leaned her blond head on his shoulder with a long sigh, "I'm very much in love with Barry but..."

"Can't we just skip the sordid details. If I told you what I wanted, you wouldn't take it the wrong way would you?".

She lifted her head off his shoulder and looked him straight in the eyes. "What do you want, Patrick?".

His voice dropped half an octave as he ventured

speculatively, mindful of not taking liberties, "Would you mind very much if I were to put two arms around you?".

She chokingly echoed a ring of nervous laughter, turned into his very receptive, trembling arms and cried softly into his shoulder while he kissed her earlobe ever so gently. Releasing her slightly he drew hard on the cigarette, then with pursed lips and tilted head he exhaled the smoke slowly through the open window, deliberating, before throwing it out with an almighty force. He could feel her eyes on his profile, watching his every move and was aware that she was identifying with him, as though mesmerised.

He switched on the cassette; the voice of a well loved male country singer reached their ears: 'Missing you, I'll never be free - from wishing you, were missing me.

"Says who?". He immediately touched fast forward till he found something more appropriate:

I guess its part of the master plan
To be tempted to fall in love again
Tem-em-pted, tem-em-pted
Tempted to fall in love again
Tem-em-pted, tem-em-pted.
I'm tempted to fall in love again.

His body shuddered next to hers as he gathered her to him; he felt they were both sharing the same unbelievable sensitivity as he whispered, "Let's both stop crying for the moon; no more tears, Jill, they're only for the lonely and life is too short to be lonely. Tonight, I want you".

"Oh, Patrick", she whispered, the seductive words of the song still ringing in their ears, "Tonight, I want you too".

She reached up her soft lips and pressed them on his ever so gently, taking his breath away. At the same time his hand strayed underneath her blouse; yes, they were supple, warm and smooth to the touch, nipples easily aroused to firmness. Her waistband was loose, he guided his fingers sensuously down between the soft cotton of her underwear and the smooth skin of her flat abdomen and beyond - My God, was she keen! But dammit! Dammit! Dammit! There was nothing he could do about it - while he had been very much alive from the waist down, he had been acting dead from the neck up! He had no protection; sure it never entered his head that he and she...

"I'm sorry, Jill, I think I'm about to take the brunt of your damnin'...".

"Oh, Patrick", she lamented, "I...".

Suddenly there was an announcement over the loudspeaker. "Would all passengers travelling to Cork on flight No ...".

"Thank God", breathed Patrick as he got to his feet, "This is one airport I'll be glad to see the backside of".

Chapter Fourteen

Barry caught the next flight to Cologne by the skin of his teeth and was on his way in a hire car to the meeting place. Never in a million years would he have connected Patrick to aiding and abetting Jill in her disappearance. He had gone through all the obvious channels of trying to find her: Maria didn't know where she was, but said if she did know she wouldn't tell him; that woman hated his guts but then she had every reason to dislike him after the way he had treated Jill in the past. His next call had been on her father; he would have helped him if he could, but was only able to convey that she rang him to say they were alright and not to worry. Michelle hadn't heard anything - God, he'd been gullible - he believed her.

He kept his eye resolutely on the road, missing things potentially interesting, as he concentrated solely on the most direct route and the landmarks Patrick told him to look out for. There seemed to be an unending traffic flow, then as he neared the locality he pulled in to go through the directions once more. He was within a few kilometres - checking the next turnings he drove off carefully, keeping a keen look out - over the bridge, right at the pub displaying the big red sign advertising Wurstchens. He jerked on his brakes as some damn stupid maniac in a high-powered Mercedes recklessly pulled right out in front of him, bashing his nearside headlight, then roared off hell for leather without stopping. Barry noted the last three digits of the registration number but knew he had time to do damn all about it. He tried to keep his concentration; first left then second right; he missed his turn off and had to go back.

At last he pulled into the park - the car Patrick described was down at the far end.

His heart thumped in anticipation of seeing her once again and hoped he wouldn't startle her. He closed his car door, locked it and headed towards hers. As yet there was no sign of her, the windows were misted over with the exception of one small area that she must have wiped for vision. As he approached he noticed that the door on the driver's side was slightly ajar - he decided to give her fair warning. "Jill! Its Barry, don't be alarmed".

He pulled back the car door swiftly and took in the situation straight away; she wasn't there. The key was in the ignition and the engine idling. He got into the car, switched off the engine and became unduly worried as he picked up three envelopes from different parts of the car, as if they had been flung recklessly in abandonment. He searched the car fully, finding her handbag tucked neatly beneath the passenger seat. He became fraught, his anxiety growing by the second, as he knew she would never have gone off without it.

He thought nothing could have been worse than when he returned to find her gone seven months ago; but at least she had gone of her own free will then, this time it bore all the hallmarks of an abduction. After locking the car he ran towards his - the coolness of the air penetrated his light clothing and he shivered as he stared ahead of him into the chill, sinister darkness of the night. He had to hurry, Frau Wedikind first, then the police.

He loved her more than he had ever loved Joanne Debussy

at the very height of their affair; he loved her more than the children; he had assumed an honourable love for them on the death of their parents but the love he had for Jill outweighed any other in his previous life. At this juncture in time he would do anything to make her happy - a flicker of doubt went through his mind and he stopped his racing thoughts to check them - Yes! His love for her was such, that he would do anything to make her happy, not do anything to get her.

The voice spoke in broken English, "Mrs Thorpe, I am sorry about the gags and knots but it won't be long now. I can also assure you that absolutely no one will come to any harm providing you do what you are told".

She had stopped struggling long ago once she realized it was ineffectual. These people had been her main reason for going into hiding and she needed all the bravado she could muster. Miki, who had on many occasions accepted her hospitality, was now the cause of her worst nightmare. He and Joanne didn't seem to be the criminal type, but then criminals are made up of all sorts of people with a passion; next door neighbours; best friends; mothers and fathers. She would die rather than hand Bonny over to them and if it came to that, these unlikely law-breakers, famous though they both were, would become murderers.

As she was whisked along, feeling sick, Miki answered the unasked questions that were flowing through her mind: "We hired a private detective to locate you and he has been following your every move now for three months and has observed your pattern; knows every one of your clientele by name; taped your phone calls to everyone including Jane Page and Michelle Edgar. Your husband and my once close associate knows nothing of your whereabouts and was very averse to calling the police. If the police are called on this occasion, Jill, it will be to your detriment".

The car pulled up at last; she didn't struggle as Miki carried her inside. Once he removed the blindfold she looked beyond him to the woman sitting quietly at the far side of the room. Gone were the good looks the world saw - Jill had never seen a woman deteriorate in such a short space of time. She still had a gracefulness about her and her voice when she spoke was as amiable and soothing as it had been on the previous occasion they had met. There was no greeting; kidnappers don't greet people. "Nothing matters to me, Jill, but my daughter. Unfortunately, I don't want her frightened so I have to put up with you as well".

"You'll never be able to kidnap Bonny! Patrick will be guarding her at this very moment". Jill knew her own voice was stony cold but that was how she felt.

"No, I will not kidnap Bonny, but you will bring her here tomorrow".

"I will not!"

"We will see".

Miki pointed to a vacant seat near Joanne saying,

"Please sit down, Jill! Coffee?".

She gazed from one to the other in bewilderment, then nodded that she would like coffee and Miki immediately left them together. She thought the way they had carried out the kidnapping was cunning but certainly not masterly; if Patrick hadn't been late they would have made a boob. Feeling cross at the way they had got her into this intolerable situation she said bluntly, "You'll never take Bonny away from me, Joanne. You may have given birth to her but she is mine now, my sole reason for breathing and I will die for her".

"That is very touching", she smiled, "But I don't think it will come to that. Things are different now, Jill, I can't have her for long. You see, I'm dying!".

Jill looked into the tired and drained face of the woman Barry had loved for so long and knew immediately she was telling the truth. She had a greyness of face and her sunken eyes were already on the brink of death.

She suddenly felt uneasy and vexed towards the condemned woman but had no control on the words that came out harshly, "You didn't have to go about this like criminals, for God's sake. Haven't you ever heard of phones and the art of negotiation?".

"I'm sorry, Jill, it was the simplest way. You must agree that if you had known I was in the vicinity you would have packed up and left. After all, you know very well I swore to Barry that I only wanted to see her once. That was all I did want you know; although she was in my mind constantly, I thought all I needed was to fulfil a natural curiosity. Then when I saw her, my life's objectives changed - I wanted her!".

It was essential that she granted this woman her dying wish otherwise she would have nothing but a gaping vacuum of nothingness left before her.

"I need to make a phone call before they call the police", said Jill.

Joanne dialled the number; she knew it off by heart.

The phone rang in Frau Wedikind's kitchen where Barry and she sat face to face across the table. Barry would have answered it but Frau Wedikind raised her hand to suppress him.

She held the phone slightly off her ear so that they could both hear. Jill's voice came clearly down the line. "I am safe and well. Please have Bonny ready and her case packed in readiness for me collecting her at 9.00am in the morning. No police to be involved and I really and truthfully mean that". The phone was replaced immediately; Barry and Frau Wedikind knew that someone else had held the phone and replaced it as soon as the message was conveyed.

Three quarters of an hour later Joanne proceeded Jill into the bedroom which was comfortable looking and warm. Before pulling back the curtains she looked out into the dark gardens then raised her eyes towards the sky which looked so peaceful with a half moon and a sprinkling of stars. "I'm looking forward to the peace, Jill, when I will have no more pain".

Jill laid her hand on her arm soothingly as she softened towards her.

"You understand, don't you, Jill, that I want her to know her real mother and not to go through life wondering what the wicked woman, who abandoned her at birth, was like".

"I understand, Joanne! Perfectly".

Joanne gave Jill an outline of her intentions: Her singing voice was fading fast and she was no longer able to compete on the operatic stage - they had been wonderfully happy and productive years for her but all she wanted now was that Bonny would have the chance to follow in her footsteps and enjoy the limelight as she had done; that she could tutor her for as long as she was able. She concluded in a business-like tone, "I emphasise that the months Bonny spends in my company will not be a sacrifice, more a substantial gain; what I can teach her and transcribe in theory will stand her in good stead".

Jill felt uneasy in the night when she heard the faint whining of the woman coming from a far corner of the house, gradually lapsing into silence.

In the silence a dreadful melancholy came over Jill and she felt inconsolably sorry for the woman who had earlier felt the first flutters of life inside her; the tiny movements that increased until she was being kicked with a force that left her feeling like a punchball. She endured the severe pains of labour and childbirth that produced no prize for the suffering. No woman, however heartless, would give up her baby without a very good reason. Joanne's reason was kept to herself and that reason tortured her for the rest of her days.

Miki drove Jill to the Wedikind's house in the morning and waited for her to collect Bonny. He remained in full view as he knew he had Jill's full cooperation and that was all he needed.

Jill let herself in and on seeing Bonny smiled broadly and held out her arms to her. She opened her mouth to speak but before she got one word out she saw him standing at the far end of the room and she was struck dumb. Nothing tangible could escape her lips, it was as if she was hit with a thunderbolt that clapped her mind. She was in no way prepared for being confronted with Barry rather than Patrick and Frau Wedikind.

Bonny was excited, "Mummy", it had been the child's decision to call her that, "Uncle Barry came to visit and stayed all night. Please, mummy, can we go back with him? Look, our cases are all packed and I can't wait to see Iain and Alan and Jamie and ...".

Her heart fell; on top of everything else, she was going to have to sort out this muddled tangle in front of the man she least wanted to see.

"No, darling, we are going somewhere else! A lovely lady is going to teach you to sing". It was a feeble and insubstantial attempt that immediately sent Bonny screaming and stamping her feet in a tantrum, saying she could sing already.

Barry took Bonny by the hand and led her into the kitchen to Frau Wedikind's open arms, saying, "I'm sorry, Frau Wedikind, but can you deal with this, Jill and I have some sorting out to do".

He returned filled with impatience and pent-up anger, the last thing he wanted was for this to erupt in an outright confrontation, but he had to try and make her see sense without seeming to knock it into her.

"I knew that Miki and Joanne had taken a well earned break from the operatic stage but this morning I suddenly remembered a press report in a newspaper last week that queried her health so I rang her physician and learnt about her terminal illness. Everything fell into place and I knew that she would want Bonny near her, at any cost, for the rest of her life. I also knew that Miki would assist in granting her dying wish. It is obvious she has won you over as well but we have to consider Bonny's feelings in the matter. Don't you think she has been deprived of her brothers long enough? It is time you brought her home".

The shock of meeting Barry without prior warning was getting to her and she felt weak and drained but tried to compose herself. "Because I am a woman I know what Joanne wants more than you and I will not break faith with her now". He caught her in his arms as the colour drained from her face and her legs buckled beneath her.

Sitting her down on the chair he lowered her head between her knees in an effort to prevent the faint. His voice was tender, "My darling, I am sorry for causing you this distress and I know you want to do what is right by Joanne but I'm sure we can work out a compromise, somehow. As I told you before, never, ever underestimate your hold over me; I love you, Jill, and I want you to come home".

The words echoed in her ears; was she hearing right in her state of half-faint? It was like as if the words were coming to her in a dream, a figment of her imagination. Even when they were close, so very close, in Devon, he had never uttered the words she so wanted to hear.

She swayed as he left her for a moment, then he was suddenly holding a glass of water to her lips and she sipped submissively.

"I have a lot of explaining to do but to cut it short, I have never loved Teresa, ever; the children were by artificial insemination. Because I knew you didn't love me I didn't see any point in advertising it until the time was right; now I want to give our marriage a chance and hopefully you will learn to love me half as much as I love you".

She looked up into his eyes as they searched deep into hers and instinctively knew, without any further surmising, that he loved her. "I overheard you say to Sir Malcolm *'She was the love of my life, we offered each other complete happiness and joy. I am still obsessed and in love with her and will be thinking of her all of my natural life"'*. She knew it word for word, it was stamped on her mind like a well learned poem.

"You overheard that? Well, I couldn't exactly let them know the children were out of a syringe; I had to let them think they were conceived with deep love and that I had as much right to them as Teresa. With hindsight, I was wrong not to confide in you".

Jill never felt more unhappy in her life; it would have been better if he hadn't loved her and a deep sense of bitterness crept over her.

He was speaking again, excitedly this time. "Bonny will be ours, there is no question about that, she will have access to her brothers, they will be more like cousins. The boys will be so excited when they know you are coming back, Jill. Iain and ...".

"No, Barry! No! ", she cut in, unable to listen to whatever he was going to say about the boys, it would be too heartbreaking, "Even if I wasn't doing this charitable deed for Joanne, I wouldn't go back to you. As soon as it is legally permissible, I want a divorce!".

His eyebrows raised and revealed a dark, quizzical expression. He was aghast and badly hurt as he slowly and shrinkingly muttered the words, "I know you don't love me, but ... you hate me that much? So much, that you won't even give it a try".

So many emotions surged through her at once; stupidity,

remorse, sacrifice, love and loathing. She dislocated herself from him and looked at him with love's eye gone cold. "No, I don't hate you, Barry. I just don't want to stay married to you". She lowered her eyes before continuing, "You see, there is someone else! There should be no complications with the divorce. I'll fall in with whatever you come up with".

She raised her eyes slowly - his chilly gaze matched hers.

Rising with a shakiness to her feet she went through to the kitchen to collect Bonny.

Saying goodbye to Frau Wedikind she told her they would meet again as she had to finish coaching a few remaining pupils.

"Auf Wiedersehen, Jill. Both you and Bonny are very welcome here", said Frau Wedikind as she kissed her.

When they reached the car Barry was reduced to tears as he kissed and hugged Bonny while she in turn clung to him like a leech. She listened as he told her that it wouldn't be long until she saw himself and her brothers once again.

Jill looked into his handsome face fleetingly before getting into the car and once again saw the love in his eyes for her, coupled with an impenetrable sadness.

He threw one final glare at Miki before slamming the car

door.

"Bastard! Bastard! Bastard!", he yelled after the car that displayed the three digits he had memorized.

Word gets around fast when it comes to Dr Barry Thorpe's movements. The place was full of photographers flashing from every angle.

"I wonder what the gutter press will dream up for this?", said Miki, in his quiet manner, "...and which one of us is a bastard?".

"I reckon it's me. Oh, Miki, why is life such a bitch?", she said, as she wiped her tears.

They barely had time to get through the door before the photographers and reporters arrived. From then on they lay in wait in pursuit of a story, never seemed to go away; perhaps they were on shifts. One young female reporter had the cheek to peer through the letter-box; the maid frightened her off by poking the brush handle through. Miki protected Joanne from peering eyes, kept the blinds at an angle so that she could see out but they couldn't see in. Jill and Miki came and went without camouflage for a week and never varied their answers to the probing questions, 'Sorry, we have nothing to say', until at last they got bored and moved on to a new scandal that was emerging. They made up some rubbish for their editors but never came back.

After she got over the first initial confusion, when she would have bolted if not restrained, Bonny settled into her new surroundings. She seemed to have an inbuilt adaptability learned through constant change and took to Miki very quickly while he in turn absolutely adored her. She resembled him in many ways, inheriting some of his physical characteristics, especially his bony, angular face. Jill also observed that her mannerisms and gestures were very similar to Joanne's.

The first real closeness between Joanne and Bonny came with the singing. When Joanne first sang Bonny was spellbound and likewise when Bonny made a playful effort Joanne hugged her saying, "Bonny, you were born to sing".

Joanne seemed to take on a new zest for living acquiring a renewed incredible courage and determination to carry on. She had been in despair at ending her life with a glass half empty, whereas now it was half full.

Miki set about writing the lyrics of a song suitable for Bonny to sing, but he did admit that words were neither here nor there without the accompanying music which Barry would have been wonderful at marrying in.

As the months went by, due to the vocal link between them, Joanne and Bonny became totally immersed in each other, while Jill and Miki became more companionable. Jill found Miki to be knowledgeable on a wide range of subjects, with a voracious intellectual curiosity, over and above music, ballet and opera, which was expected of him. Joanne hated to dwell on the past but gave in to letting him write her biography. She reminisced right back to her childhood on things so long repressed.

The most difficult part of the book for Miki to write and accept was that Barry had been the love of her life and that he himself had been a fling that she could never quite shake off.   Barry had been hurt at the end of their relationship due to hurt pride rather than broken-heartedness.   In all their years together he never once asked her to marry him and it was all she wanted to do. Joanne had thought that the separation she had initiated between them would have made him realize he wanted to marry her, instead his feelings for her diminished completely.

Miki asked Jill's permission to mention Bonny in the biography and she could see no reason to keep it secret.

Joanne told them that the only reason for the fabrication of Bonny's parentage was in the hope that Barry would do the honourable thing and marry her, but he didn't.

Chapter Fifteen

Eamon called lethargically to Michelle, "Patrick has just pulled up outside".

She hurried into the hall, chanting instructions in the event of Becky wakening, while pulling on her jacket. "Try her with the dummy first, if that doesn't work, I've left a bottle of juice in the fridge".

A sharp toot of a horn sounded. "I wish you would tell him, Michelle, it's not fair on Patrick".

She kissed him but didn't answer as she slipped through the door. It was easy to let things drift; Patrick had a magnetic hold on her and she dreaded the thought of losing him. The bad part about severing with a lover, if he could ever have been called that, was, that everything good in the relationship had to stop as well and there was a lot good between Patrick and she. He had the capability of lifting her out of the doldrums into high spirits as no one else on earth.

Eamon watched as Patrick played a prank on her at the car and his heart sank. He was almost certain she was in love with him now, but this man, Patrick O'Rafferty, had something unique that women went for in a big way.

"Bye, Patrick, I really enjoyed myself tonight", said Michelle as she pounced out of the car.

"No kisses tonight then?", asked Patrick, lowering his

head to look at her before she slammed the door. They had laughed their sides sore at the hilarious show, 'One Hell of a Do', in which Jon Kenny and Pat Shortt acted out a brilliant mixture of music and comedy in the Everyman Palace. Afterwards they prattled excitedly about it as they wolfed down some sticky doughnuts on the way back to the car.

"Oh, Patrick, I'm sorry", she said, about to jump back into the car but he got out and went round to her side. He held her by the upper arms with gentle pressure and just as she was about to kiss him, he said, "How long are we going to continue with, your words, this habit, Michelle? I reckon this could run on for twenty years, just like my Uncle Liam and Breda Walsh. What do you reckon?".

"I'd like it to continue for ever, Patrick".

"We can't have our cake and eat it. Sorry, Michelle, we've got to call a halt sometime. I'm in love with someone else!", he raised his eyes and looked beyond her to the outline of Eamon in the window, "...and I think you have someone who loves you as well".

Michelle breathed a sigh of relief, it was horrible and final but the weight had lifted at last. She lowered her head, leaned it against his strong chin and with a tear in her eye, she said, "Things never worked out for us, Patrick, we were simply cut out to be good friends, but this woman you love is so lucky she couldn't go far wrong with you; nobody could".

Patrick was sad as well and returned the tribute, "God

knows Eamon has had it tough, but he has been lucky to find someone like you".

Chapter Sixteen

It was Friday evening and Patrick made his way to visit Teresa as he had been doing now for months. His mind was chock-full of her and the love he felt for her was tremendous; he had never dreamt that any one woman could have such a hold on him. Without her life wouldn't be worth a twopenny farthing piece and the sun would never rise again. He smiled as he had the romantic musings. If it hadn't been for a little peasant girl named Helga he could very well have gone through the whole of his life not knowing he was really a romantic at heart. It was a nice feeling knowing that she was his and his alone and he wasn't sharing her with anyone, however, he would never be able to ask her to marry him due to hollow feelings of frustration and inadequacy.

It was six days since he had last been with her as he had been on a business trip to the Mosel.

"Oh, Patrick, I will miss you so much, how I wish I could go with you. Will you please tell Karl Heinz and Frau Braemer that I love them and hope it won't be long till we all meet up again".

As he left he plucked her cheek affectionately, saying, "Cheer up, it's only five days".

Patrick knew only too well, as sure as God made little green apples, a lot can and does happen in five days. He thought over the third night of his stay in the Mosel.

"Seen anything of Jill?", asked Patrick, as he drained the

last of the delightful concoction Frau Wedikind had made up for him. On the previous occasion he had been in the Mosel she had just been settling in with Miki Delecour and Joanne Debussy so he decided not to bother her.

"Yes, Pat. I see her every week. She and Bonny are fine, just fine".

"Would you mind letting me have her address, I'd like to go and see her while I'm in the area", said Patrick.

"I wouldn't, if I were you, Pat. You have done your duty by her, just let things be", said Frau Wedikind fingering her glass nervously.

"I must see her! I need to satisfy myself that she is alright".

"She is very tied up with those people she's staying with and from what she tells me, the singer is failing fast and they are making more and more demands on her".

Patrick snapped his fingers impatiently, "Out with it; I'm not leaving the Mosel without seeing her".

Frau Wedikind wrote out the address. ''I personally think it would be better if you left Jill to sort out her own life and devote your time to the lovely Hel.. Teresa, whom you are obviously so very much in love with".

He had driven to the gates of the house Miki Delecour had taken to rent. It was tucked in a private non-residential area away from the public roads, the ornate gates securely locked. He parked his car, climbed the fence and walked up the lengthy, impressive tree-lined and well lit drive as the journalists did all those months ago. It was a perfect haven for people who wished to get away from it all. As it was an unusually warm and balmy night in June a light coating of perspiration had formed on his upper lip when at last the house came into view. The delicate fragrance of the scented summer flowering shrubs in the air reminded him of Jill. Enthused, he took a quick intake of breath and hurried his step.

Miki answered the door and after he had inspected his credentials, asked Patrick to step in. The vestibule was bright and airy, the temperature pleasant due to the air conditioning. "Jill is with Miss Debussy, she will be down shortly. I am fixing a meal, Mr O'Rafferty, would you care to join us?".

"No, thank you. As soon as I see Jill, I'll be on my way".

Miki led him through to the kitchen where he had obviously assumed the role of chef.

"We know all about you, Mr O'Rafferty, we had you thoroughly investigated and of course Jill has spoken of you to us but I will have to double-check that she wishes to see you".

Patrick felt uneasy as Miki spoke to Jill on the phone. Going by the one sided phone conversation, she obviously had reservations about meeting him. Surely she wasn't bothered about the last time they had been together and what had happened between them - he had put it out of his mind and was certain she would have too. At last she agreed to see him.

Patrick waited impatiently to see her after the long separation; she seemed an age. Miki offered him a whisky while he waited. He refused.

At long last she stepped into the kitchen and completely blew his mind - she had a ravishing radiance about her and he was instantly reminded of how she felt in his arms. His eyes fell on her breasts that were full, supported by a bra, they would be supple, warm and smooth to the touch. Her abdomen; oh how he longed to run his hands over her abdomen, feel her silky skin; her blond hair shone and her skin was blooming. Her steady gaze held his as she uttered demurely, "Hello, Patrick".

He couldn't reply; the woman had left him gobsmacked and perplexed - a tear rolled from his eye - 'I'd never cry Da, if it wasn't for the women'. Eventually he got some words out. "Would you mind, Mr Delecour, if I have that whisky after all and make it a double".

He drove to the front of Checkerberry and became excited with longing for the woman within. "Sorry, Mrs Thorpe, no doubt you will enhance my thoughts again, but", he whispered, "just now, inside this grand house, a very ravishing lady with black hair and velvety skin, is waiting to be served".

Patrick checked his watch as they lay side by side in the enormously, extravagant and comfortable bed that had previously been occupied by Sir Malcolm and Lady Sylvia. It was an unusual bed, a symbol of great wealth; the material was silk, richly and elaborately embroidered. This bed was designed as a source of great pleasure and he doubted if Sir Malcolm and Lady Sylvia would have put the energy, passion and sexy high jinks onto the mattress supported on the iron frame, concealed by drapes, that he and Teresa did. He smiled as he leaned on his elbow and looked into her peaceful face. Her longing for him never failed to delight and excite him. After they had made love tonight, between the second and third time, she shocked him by saying, "Pat O'Rafferty, do you intend stringing me along for twenty years like that daft old Uncle of yours? I want to bring the whole thing out into the open; I absolutely hate you coming here after the children have gone to bed, then scarpering before they are up in the morning; I want to tell my parents about us; to simplify it: I want to marry you! Think carefully before you speak, Pat O'Rafferty, as I'm likely to kick you out of my bed and never let you squeak the springs again if you don't fall in with my wishes".

It wasn't a subject Patrick could treat lightly - it was a serious situation and he felt his life was disintegrating around him; there was no way he could ever marry her. "If I could marry you, my darling, I would be the happiest man alive, but I'm sad to say we simply can't ever end up as man and wife".

"Why; Pat, why?", she cried frantically.

"I thought it was obvious, my darling. You are way, way above my class! How could I ever keep you in the manner to which you are accustomed. I lead a very modest life style with a similarly modest income?"

She became very cross and screamed at him, "You stupid, stupid, idiot! My love for you, Pat, outweighs everything else I possess; bricks and mortar, landscaped gardens, fancy clothes are useless without your love".

"You will always have that love, my darling, I could swear that on a stack of Bibles; I am not suddenly going to rob you of it simple because I won't marry you. If we were to marry, you would miss your type of lifestyle in no time at all and maybe even stop loving me because I deprived you of it".

"Pat O'Rafferty, have you not heard me accurately? I am willing to contemplate a complete change of lifestyle and status to be your wife", she said exasperated.

He arched his brows to reveal a gaze that was sceptical. "Would you uproot yourself and your children from here, marry me and come to live in my house?".

"I would uproot myself and my children to live in a mud hut with you, where there was plenty of fresh air, spring water and wild animals".

He would live in a mud hut with her as well, so what the hell! He had an insatiable appetite for this woman, accordingly he manoeuvred her naked body until it lay on top of him.

As she lay on top of him, his penetration deep, she knew

there was no way in the world that she could ever do without him, he was a way of life to her now, whether they got married or not.

His gasping words were music in her ears, "I wonder if this is unique, accepting a proposal of marriage while on the job and keeping up a conversation. I'll marry you, my darling, but I'm not going to uproot you. I'll sell my estate, put the money into the upkeep of this place while you join me in the wine trade, after all you demonstrated your flair for it when you worked for Karl Heinz in the Mosel. Who knows, you might have inherited some of your father's financial genius. Just think - O'Rafferty's Wine Empire".

"Oh, Pat, I don't know! I sort of liked the idea of the mud hut".

He ran his tongue around her tongue, along her teeth until she bit him; he liked it. "In fifteen minutes flat, my sweetheart, I'm going to drag Iain and Alan out of bed and tell them who their new dad is going to be. Jamie has a flute exam in the morning so I'll leave him to get a good night's sleep".

"Keep quiet, Pat O'Rafferty, I want to concentrate".

She was fulfilled, happy and tired when she rolled from his body down into the bed and just before falling asleep, muttered, "Even you wouldn't be that daft, Pat O'Rafferty".

As she lay asleep, Patrick checked his watch again and got

out of bed, tucked the clothes around her tenderly then went to wake up Iain and Alan. "Get those blears out of your eyes boys - there is American Football on the tele' - the St Louis Cardinals are playing the New York Giants".

May as well start this father-figure business the way he intended to go on - by laying down the law.

Chapter Seventeen

The bearded, silver-haired and bespectacled gentleman in his sixties, reserved in manner, made his way home up a narrow twisting lane; his body seemed to unwind with each step. The hedgerows on each side of the road were brimming with colourful wild flowers. He wondered to himself how one could live for so long in the same house and location and yet every day in life look upon his surroundings as if he was seeing it for the first time with a fresh eye. There were times though, when he was deep in thought, he didn't hear the sound of the waves lashing below - today they filled his ears and he felt happy - no not happy, gratified, with his lot.

He was carrying his little bag from the local shop in one hand containing just one trout and one stick of bread while holding his newspaper up under his arm with the other. He walked past the thatched cottage on the bend with the low stone wall and a rackety little gate that added a certain country charm. The gardens were always neat and tidy, laid out in lawns and roses; the agency certainly looked after the place well. He could never pass without looking, it sometimes brought a lump to his throat and he wondered what type of people would be taking it this year.

It was a lonely life but he was resigned to it now. He had made a few new friends since Alice had encouraged him to join the art society. She thought that by getting involved it might take his mind off his troubles - he took to it like a duck to water and it had a real therapeutic function by increasing his curiosity and creative instincts as he was now always looking for ways to express his pictorial skills.

Rounding the next bend his own little cottage came into view - it held a fascination of its own but seemed so still and quiet; There was no one to welcome him; never again would that familiar voice call, "That you?". It was one year and nine months now since she died but he always felt the same. Would this ambience stay with him till the end of his days?

He shuffled up the path, the pain in his knee always got worse at this stage, it seemed to know it was time for a rest. He found the key in his pocket, fitting it in the lock he opened the door then walked inside closing it behind him. After he had deposited his trout in the fridge he settled down in front of the hearth giving the fire a stir with the poker then, changing over his spectacles, sat back to read his newspaper.

There was the sound of a heavy car pulling up outside; he curiously leaned back, looked out of the window and saw a taxi idling. A woman with a child got out; he observed that the woman paying the taxi driver was pregnant but his glasses were out of focus and he couldn't see clearly. Damn! Where had he laid down his distance spectacles? My God, he thought in a panic, the taxi was moving off leaving the heavily pregnant woman and child stranded with heavy suitcases at the wrong house.

She picked up one of the cases and told Bonny to go ahead and open the gate. Bonny was excited and skipped happily up the path and was about to ring the quaint little bell when the door opened wide and a man appeared waving his spectacles about. He put them on and looked beyond the child to his beautiful and heavily pregnant daughter struggling with a heavy case. His throat tightened and the tears spilled over as he held out his arms to her.

She went into them and they cried together. Then sniffing she moved out of his arms and said, "Father, I've come home for the time being to sort myself out. There is nowhere else on this earth I want to be, but if you don't want me in this condition, I'll leave you in peace - but please, could it be tomorrow?".

Without saying a word, he walked past her up the path to get the other case; he was crying so much, he was too choked to speak.

He pulled himself together once they were inside and held out his hand to the beautiful little girl with the black shining hair. "So this is Bonny, I presume. I'm your Grandpa! I can't wait to take you on the beach, my girl - there's a donkey tethered up not far from here - tomorrow you can have a ride on it. Then the next day I will take the car out of the garage and we will go through the natural sub-tropical gardens at Overbecks; get ice cream. Next week we will ...".

Jill slumped her overburdened body into the chair in exhaustion; she had been accepted, but would soon hear the sharp edge of his tongue because he was an honourable man with a strong social conscience and expected his family to live up to his high principles. She could almost hear what he would say now - 'sure the world is going to the dogs'.

Bonny had already accepted her new Grandpa; if ever a little girl was acquiescent it was she. "Grandpa, you can throw this old badge away because I've got a new one", she said proudly and pressed the old badge into his hand.

He turned it over and smiled as he said, "But this badge looks like new! Are you sure you don't want it any more?".

"Yes, I am certain I don't want it". she said with a gurgling laugh, "It would be silly. Will you pin this new one on for me?".

Jill watched attentively as her father pinned the badge on Bonny's lapel.

"Do you mind if I have this lovely badge? It's too good to throw away".

Bonny nodded imposingly and became very engrossed as she reached out to his lapel. "I'll help pin it on, Grandpa".

When the badge was secured, Jill's father winked at her, as he said, "Look at our new badges mummy: I am five and Bonny is six".

She looked at the two badges and smiled broadly; her father and Bonny were going to be good for each other.

As he helped them unpack he thought of his supper: If he was to look towards the heavens and give thanks to the good Lord for sending forth his daughter and Bonny, while breaking up the stick of bread, would it increase threefold, together with the trout.

"Father! Look!", Jill said excitedly holding up the instrument, "I've brought my flute!".

He looked at her with happiness in his heart. Her morals may have slipped but she was his little girl and they were on the same wavelength, sharing an intense specific affinity. The gratification he had felt earlier had only been a secret hope of greater things to come, such as happiness.

Chapter Eighteen

Sir Malcolm replaced the phone then straight away spoke on the intercom to his secretary. "Miss Foster, I do not want to be disturbed for fifteen minutes by yourself or anyone else".

"Very well, Sir Malcolm".

He had some thinking and sorting out to do in his mind, as he picked up and replaced his fountain pen; picked it up again then started to tap-tap-tap on his desk pad repeatedly. Drat this miserable business of O'Rafferty, he thought violently, how dare the bastard have the audacity to ask Teresa to marry him; worse still, how dare Teresa consider the proposal; says she intends to marry the practically penniless bugger.

Damn children nowadays! They cause more problems than enough and right through to maturity. The coming of age was lowered to eighteen: They wanted to vote; leave home; get married; spend our hard earned cash; but at the end of the day they end up acting like juveniles at the age of thirty plus. We took heed of our parents until we were twenty one, thereafter assumed complete responsibility for our lives, while still respecting them. Teresa was about to show them up by not learning to distinguish between people; Patrick wasn't exactly the epitome of distinction that warranted marrying someone of her worth although there was no doubt the children took kindly to his sharp wit. He was a cheerful and decent enough fellow and he had indeed held him in considerable respect, but not as a son-in-law; no, never as a son-in-law. Although he was not completely impoverished, had a little business, the whole idea of it was wholly impractical.

Teresa had said to him just now on the phone that Patrick was in London on business and would like both of us to get together for a friendly chat, man to man. He looked at the number he had just scribbled, 0831.... a mobile which Patrick had taken on transient hire service. He would have a friendly chat alright! Put a stop to the ridiculous nonsense! Pay off the bugger who was suffering from delusions of grandeur, his type would never be able to resist it.

He would leave Lady Sylvia out of this as she had a soft spot for the Irishman. The damn man was the type who could break the rules and get away with it. Once, on her birthday, Patrick had been in the kitchen delivering wine when young Alan presented her with a card he had designed personally. Iain stood bowed and said, "I would have made you one but I thought you might have kissed me for it". Patrick stood forward as she flushed slightly and boldly said, "A beautiful lady deserves to be kissed on her birthday; allow me?". She held out her cheek, he side-stepped it and gave her a mighty smacker on the mouth. The smile never left her face for hours.

Yes! this was a man to man deal; he dialled the number... 'The vodophone you have called may be switched off. Please try later'.

"Miss Foster, will you try this number every fifteen minutes until you get through. It's urgent! The number is ...".

Miss Foster deposited the large envelope on Sir Malcolm's desk. "I've counted it twice: Two hundred thousand pounds in fifty pound notes. Shall that be all, Sir Malcolm?".

Sir Malcolm patted the envelope that would cast O'Rafferty swiftly into ignominy, where his daughter was concerned, answered her confidently, "Yes, Miss Foster. When Mr O'Rafferty arrives I want no disturbance short of... well, short of another black/white/multi-coloured Wednesday".

Patrick announced himself; he was by no means the usual jack-in-office type, then she had a hunch he wouldn't be. He was - well, different - hair flopping down over his cheek and with a certain self-confident and light-hearted mood that actually brought a smile to her face. In the four minutes that Sir Malcolm kept him waiting, he effortlessly entertained her. She liked the devil in his eyes, his spontaneous Irish prattle - and she liked him.

"Patrick", Sir Malcolm greeted him, "Lovely to see you".

"Lovely to see you also, Sir Malcolm".

The handshake was fleeting, weak and watery.

"Glad you were able to see me, Patrick. How is business?"

Patrick knew the conversation would go through this desultory preliminary before the big issue.

"Not too bad - the recession has been deep but confidence is gradually seeping through and it is picking up surprisingly".

Sir Malcolm, after a few taps on his desk pad and a few swivels in his chair, commenced speaking.

"Patrick - Teresa rang me this morning to relay your plans to marry. Far be it from me to meddle or raise objections, but, in my opinion, I don't think it is the best idea you've both ever had".

"I beg your pardon, Sir Malcolm. Am I hearing right?"

"Well, unless you are illiterate or have bad hearing, I reckon you are hearing right".

"In what way would you say it was a bad idea, Sir Malcolm, and on what basis do you make your judgement?".

"Simply because you unearthed my daughter, it doesn't exactly give you the right to marry her. To simplify it: when she kissed you it didn't mean you would necessarily change from a frog into a prince".

"God forbid that I would ever be a prince", said Patrick with a cheeky glint in his eye, "A lucky leprechaun, maybe, but not a prince, I'm just not egocentric enough". He paused, as he sought and acquired inspiration, before resuming confidently. "Sir Malcolm, you may be a financial wizard but you don't know a damn thing about human relationships. I class myself as a straight down the middle of the road man, proud of my culture. I am not self indulgent, just an ordinary, simply-educated person who feels he has the right that radical faith be put in him. My way of thinking is: Social injustice should be eradicated to bring about a society in which no one need feel inferior. We can't all be Cadillac drivers, nor wish to be. It would be too bad if a man was to be thwarted from the joys of being a lover simply because he had little means".

Sir Malcolm wasn't put off by his hypothesising; the financial wizardry in him would win the day; the power was in the envelope. He picked up and laid down his fountain pen three times before reaching into the drawer on the right hand side of his desk.

"I would say, Patrick, that you are a shrewd and prudently, sensible businessman. In this envelope I have a certain amount of money that will be very hard for you to refuse. All I ask in return is that you cut your coat according to your cloth and do well by marrying the girl you got pregnant - Yes! I know all about how you got your oar in there too - and leave my daughter to marry the man who fathered her children".

"Money does not rank highly on my list of priorities but simply out of curiosity, how much is there in the envelope, Sir Malcolm?"

"Two hundred thousand pounds. More money than you would get in five years of transporting wine about".

The eyes of the two men became locked. Sir Malcolm

was in this business a mite too long not to recognize a certain gleam stealing into Patrick's intense gaze.

The Irishman's words were slow and accentuated as he uttered, "Two..'undred..t'ousand..pounds".

He then sprawled out lankily in the chair, dramatically taking his time before speaking further, in a controlled verbosity. "Le'me see now; in this day and age, it would just about buy a house: I would need a further two 'undred t'ousand pounds to ameliorate my business before I would consider doing a deal". Two hundred thousand was just too big a figure for him to get his tongue round the correct English.

He watched Sir Malcolm play with his fountain pen for a full minute before he reached over and spoke into the phone. "Miss Foster, will you come in please?". He quickly opened the drawer on the left hand side, extricated a cheque book and commenced filling in the sum Patrick had requested.

Patrick grinned to himself, the ruthless bugger must be a multi-millionaire, he could have asked for more.

Miss Foster came in and Sir Malcolm handed her the cheque, "I want this in whatever order of notes that are available".

"I'd like fives, if possible, ...please", said Patrick, might as well make it awkward.

Sir Malcolm relaxed, the atmosphere which had been

tense and uncertain began to calm. When the deal was through, Patrick stood up and offered his hand. This time Sir Malcolm shook it excessively, and Patrick strolled out of the office with the two large envelopes, one twice as thick as the other.

He let himself into Miss Foster's office. "Miss Foster, would you mind if I asked you to type out a note of thanks for Sir Malcolm?"

"Not at all, Mr O'Rafferty, I would be delighted, in fact. What would you like me to type?".

Patrick scribbled out a note and handed it to her, then sat down to wait. He ignored the 'No Smoking' sign and lit up but would have put it out immediately if he had been asked; his nerves needed stabilising; there was a lot of money in those envelopes.

He watched as she typed; "I like your blouse, Miss Foster, especially the little pearl buttons".

She flushed to his ribbing as she typed the words, then keyed in the command to send it to the printer.

"Read it through carefully, Mr O'Rafferty, and should you decide to change the wording, I will be very pleased indeed to modify it. When you are fully satisfied, please sign it".

He read it through quickly -   Sir Malcolm - *Thank you for everything. I apologise for all the trouble I have caused you today and am very likely to cause you in future years. Please stick the four hundred thousand pounds as far up your arse as is possible. You may apply for access to your grandchildren by going through the normal channels of procedure. Good luck to your goodself and convey my very good wishes to Lady Sylvia. Your very affectionate son-in-law to be. Pat O'Rafferiy.*

He signed it. "Very nicely typed indeed, Miss Foster. I appreciate the difficulty you had.   Good day to you".

She simply had to shake the Irishman by the hand and took the initiative, while beaming a rare smile.

He picked up the envelopes and kissed them one after the other, "Sorry, we have to part company so soon; shame we hadn't time to become acquainted".

He sang the words softly 'a-nd he won the heart of a la-a-ady' to the tune of 'The Gypsy Rover' as he walked towards the lift.

Miss Foster left the bulging envelopes on Sir Malcolm's desk, "Mr O'Rafferty has left a note of thanks'', and hurried out.

He was a very well liked Chairman, but when things didn't go his way he made life hell for the staff.   She waited for her door to burst open but couldn't believe her ears when she heard the roars of laughter coming from his office.

Sir Malcolm just couldn't stop laughing. Well, he thought to himself, I tremble for my little girl's future but the Irish idiot must love her and that can't be bad.

Miss Foster wasn't exactly in the clear just yet. He stormed out of his office and burst into hers. "I'd like to remind you of your position, Miss Foster. You are my very personal, private and confidential, secretary! That understood?".

"Yes indeed, Sir. Perfectly!".

Chapter Nineteen

All eyes were on him as he slowly strolled up the church and took a seat in the middle of the empty fourth pew. He responded with a nod of the head to the familiar faces of dignitaries, composed into gravity and grief, conforming with the occasion. It had saddened him to learn of Joanne Debussy's death, but she wasn't his main reason for being here.

The coffin lay draped near the altar, his eyes lingered on it for a second then ascended to the colourful gleaming stained glass window. Jill had chosen glass like that for their front door - he could see her now, her light blue eyes shining as she ran her fingertips over the lustrous glass. He closed his eyes to block out things that reminded him of her - behind the darkness of his eyelids - she smiled at him.

He was travel-weary and suffering from jet lag that had sneaked up on him like a hang-over, having only just arrived back from Tokyo, the last port of call on his tour, five hours previously. The trip had left him drained; it had been the first time in his career that he had appeared to angry cat-calling. His career was taking a pounding but he was beyond caring - he just felt sorry for the people who had paid out their hard earned money to listen to his screwed up load of cr... "Good Afternoon, Dr Thorpe, I'm very pleased you could make it".

Although the voice was just above a whisper, it seemed like thunder in the solemn death-like silence. He turned and looked into the drained face of Miki Delecour who had settled himself beside him. The church was only two-thirds full, why the hell did he have to set his ass beside him?

He didn't greet the man but in as hushed a voice as he could manage he asked, "Where is Jill?". It was his main reason for being here. He had kept in touch with the children while on tour and they never mentioned any other man in Jill's life. For some reason she had deluded him and now that he was back he intended to find out why.

"She went home to Devon to give birth to her baby".

The burst of sound from the organ saved him from being the one to break the silence. "You bloody bastard, Delecour, you couldn't keep your filthy hands off her, just as you couldn't keep them off Joanne".

The select congregation broke into song 'Peace, Perfect Peace'. Delecour sang very loud and full-throatedly to mask the sound should there be a further barrage of words from Barry. There wasn't - he stole a sideways glance; the man was in a deep state of shock, trembling like a leaf that would fall off at any second. When the music was approaching the crescendo, he said quickly, "The bun was in the oven before she got my length".

He couldn't have wounded him with more hurtful words. Barry felt violent - That bastard O'Rafferty! As he visualized them together he blared, "Christ Almighty!", piercingly and lamentingly into the descending silence.

As all eyes sought him out and rested on him, Miki put

his arm across his shoulder and forced him down-down-down into a kneeling position; after a while their whispers gravitated solemnly to the floor.

"She never mentioned anything to us - just got bigger and bigger as the months went by. In the end she conceded and allowed us to call a doctor to make sure the baby was alright. She told us O'Rafferty was the father. I'll never forget the look on Patrick O'Rafferty's face when he saw her; his eyes fell on her enormous swollen abdomen and he was reduced to tears. I must hand it to O'Rafferty - he did the decent thing and asked her to marry him; she refused.

"I had grown fond of the girl myself and with Joanne being on the brink of death, I later threw my hat in the ring, but to no avail".

Barry tried to keep back the tears by blowing his nose into his handkerchief with the most masculine thunderous sound, not exactly suited to a place of worship. When he reinstated his handkerchief he whispered in monologue, "Her mother never liked me, you know, she was an old witch, clairvoyant they call it; knew I'd ruin her life. Well, Mrs Ashton, you got it wrong; O'Rafferty ruined your daughter's life and she ruined mine, because there is no way I would lay a finger on her again knowing that O'Rafferty had been there! I wish to hell I'd never clapped eyes on her or set foot in Devon!".

There wasn't a dry eye in the congregation, they were overcome with sympathy for him and Miki Delecour. Neither of them were considered able enough to deliver the eulogy therefore a much loved and respected member of the Opera Society fulfilled that role.

"Mr Delecour - Dr Thorpe", a very soft and soothing, feminine voice whispered between them, "I know it is a very sad day for you both but would you please rest these lilies on Miss Debussy's coffin".

Miki very obediently went forward and dropped his lily on the coffin; Barry followed and did likewise.

"The coffin is ready for burial now. Will you both lend a shoulder?".

They set off to walk, the coffin resting easily on each of their shoulders, jointly with the other four pall bearers who were also connected with the Operatic Society.

When it was lowered into the ground they stood together quietly, tears in their eyes, paying their last respects to the woman with the beautiful golden voice whom they had both loved; the voice, locked forever in the coffin, never to be heard live again.

After they had made their way through a barrage of handshakes from kindly mourners, Barry invited Miki home to spend the night.

The house was warm and inviting after their long drive. The housekeeper had left out a selection of cold meats together with cheese, fruit and a bottle of Barry's favourite Halbtrocken wine.

Miki and he ate ravenously as they sat in front of the fire.

"This is the nicest sort of meal, all it needs is a woman", said Miki in a broken voice

"I'm sorry about Joanne, Miki. Really sorry".

Miki snuffled then followed Barry's gaze to Jill's picture and felt at one with the great discomfort and sorrow that he was living through - every time he entered this room he would probably look at that face, study it intensely, while inside - he would be dying.

"I'm sorry, for us both", said Miki.

Later, while drowning their sorrows they read the coverage of the funeral in the first edition of the morning paper. It was laughable how the press got the main issues correct but made up the details in between.

It read - *The funeral service for Dame Joanne Debussy was held today at St Martin's Somerset, at 2.30pm. Inside the church, the two men most prominent in her life sat side by side, united in their sorrow. Dr Barry Thorpe was outwardly heartbroken and was unable to suppress a howl at one stage. Mr Delecour consoled him and they remained on their knees in prayer for the rest of the service. Together they laid white lilies on her coffin. Then as 1000 people watched silently, many weeping, they carried her coffin one hundred yards to the burial ground.*

The Opera House grieved for perhaps the greatest soprano singer of all time. Miss Debussy was exquisite but could

not lay claim to being a sex symbol. Her appeal lay entirely in the mysterious quality of her singing voice. She is survived by a six year old daughter, who is rumoured to possess the talent to follow in her footsteps.

As music lovers know, Miss Debussy, was discovered and nurtured by Dr Thorpe and they made a dazzling partnership. She became closely associated with Miki Delecour, a lyricist and close friend of Dr Thorpe's, who broke up the long standing romance when he fathered Miss Debussy's daughter. Recently, however, they astounded the world by all coming together in a strange arrangement of playing mixed doubles. Dr Thorpe and his now estranged wife, thought to be pregnant by Miki Delecour, are adoptive parents of Miss Debussy's daughter. Her Majesty The Queen made Miss Debussy a Dame, Commander of the British Empire, in recognition of her services to music.

Barry spoke cynically as he drained his glass. "I'm a has been, the only thing I feel like composing is a final song dedicated to Mrs Thorpe. What lyrics do you think you could come up with for this, Miki? 'I've never needed Anyone'.

He sat down at the piano and strummed a tune.

"You are compelled to compose, Barry. You must share your talent with the many fans who adore and appreciate your music. There is no real competition to the live performances of your contemporary works".

"I won't be missed; music lovers have plenty of wonderful

music by the old school of composers to thrill them. I can't ever compose again, it's lost its enchantment for me and my audiences. You weren't there, Miki, I got insults from one furious audience who kept demanding their money back. The theatre manager said nothing like it ever happened before. My music was flat, consisted of a series of toneless lack-lustre dirges. Who wants to pay good money to hear that; there was better music at the funeral today going for free. I can assure you that if the audience had access to eggs I would surely have been pelted. With the exception of a few still-faithful waverers, it was the most confusing situation I have ever been in. No, my peak has been reached, I am sadly on the way out".

"No, Barry! No! Your ability to produce memorable performances may have temporarily waned but the genius is still in there. You can't deliver because the other parts of your life are at a low ebb. No one's private life could take the bashing yours has done without some creaking, but your credibility isn't wrecked yet".

"I really mean it, Miki, I will play and enjoy music because I can't live without it, but I will never compose or play the piano to an audience in public again". In an expression of weakness and tipping the whisky bottle over his glass, he added, "I quit!".

"For heaven's sake don't quit! That would be the complete recipe for self destruction. Take a rest from it - get yourself revitalised. You are probably right when you say that your worst made them despair - So what the hell? They will forgive you anything when you reappear at your

best. You and I can do great things together; I need you
as much as you need me and don't forget, we share a
daughter waiting in the sidelines to be famous. Joanne
envisioned us both giving to Bonny as we gave to her".

"Don't bank on it, Miki, the critics are in agreement with
me, I am stuck in the plug hole on the way to the sewer".

Miki was indeed saddened as Barry had always seemed
superhuman in the way he dealt with a moment's
carelessness or a false intonation; avoiding the
temperamental weaknesses of most artists and rose above
what critics said of him.

Next day Barry took the 5.15pm flight from Heathrow to
Cork; he intended making an unsociable call on the
biggest liar in Bantry.

He picked up a hire-car at the airport and set off to meet
Patrick. He passed a large sign on the roadside
advertising the wine warehouse - *For Quality Wines,
consult Patrick O'Rafferty, the smiling, friendly, Wine
Importer, at 'The Lucky Leprechaun'. 100 yards on the
left.*

Barry breathed, "Patrick O'Rafferty, you obnoxious
prevaricator, I am going to knock that friendly smile off
your face".

CLOSED 6.00pm - Where would he go from here? Ah,
Teresa would know how to reach him, she ordered wine
from him. He drove around aimlessly for some time

before spotting a telephone kiosk. He dialled her number and got the shock of his life.

"Hello! Patrick O'Rafferty here!".

God Almighty! Think of the devil! "It's you I want O'Rafferty, but did I dial the wrong number?".

"If you dialled Teresa's number, you got it right first time. You see, Barry, Teresa and I are to be married next week and I've moved in".

"You mean to tell me that every time I visit Teresa and my children, I am going to come into contact with you as well. You must be joking!".

"Joking aside, you are absolutely right, that's about the height of it. You are half an hour away from here, Barry, so we will hold the champagne till you get here. We were just about to celebrate the birth of my son".

Teresa and the boys were waiting for him outside as he drove up. He kissed her on the cheek and spoke to each boy devotedly in turn. While he had been on tour they seemed to have grown inches. "Oh, I have missed you all so much while I have been away. I am not doing any more touring, the older I get the less I want to roam, so I'll have more time to be with you. I promise we shall have that fishing holiday very soon".

Iain said, excitedly, "Uncle Barry, guess what? Jill and Bonny are coming for a visit in three week's time and are bringing the new baby. Bonny has told us over the phone that the baby has big, big, feet and he is going to be a footballer. Patrick has big feet and he is ace at kicking the ball high; he is the baby's dad, you know!".

"Uncle Barry", Alan very quickly had his say, "Patrick doesn't want us to go to boarding school, he wants us to go to his old school - they play a lot of games there; Gaelic football, rugger and a lot of table tennis; we will have a good chance of winning the Bantry Junior Cup, as he did".

They ran off to their computer games leaving Barry to cool down. "So - Patrick is going to mould my children into little sportsmen?".

"I think it is a good idea, Barry. With the exception of Jamie, they are never going to be musicians and I do so very much want to have them close. It is our belief that their unique potential will come to the fore in the friendly and disciplined atmosphere of the local school and be more adaptable without all the outward trappings of class. I never want my children to lose their sense of community or be part of the class ridden society that is killing our culture. My parents sent me away, I've never thanked them for it. Please say you will agree?".

Barry felt that more real effort should have been put in so that Iain and Alan would get to know and like contemporary and classical music. He put his arm around her shoulder and looked into her pleading eyes. O'Rafferty was gradually moulding her into his way of thinking by palming off his reformatory political views. "It is my intention that Jamie attend Chetham's Musical

School of Excellence for a few years later on, but as for Alan and Iain, it looks as if the decision has been taken out of my hands". He moved his head slowly from side to side as he added with just a touch of scepticism, "I just hope it all works out to their advantage".

"Everything will be alright, I know it will".

He felt sorry for Teresa, she was in the same position as himself. How did she feel about Patrick making love to another woman?

"How much do you know about Patrick and Jill?".

"Everything! I know everything from the first genial arm around her shoulder to the badly timed fractionally late withdrawal that left little Patrick behind. I have been left sterile by the accident and I can't wait to hold Patrick's child in my arms. Jill has promised us access to him".

The woman loved O'Rafferty alright, it was so damned obvious. She would stand by her man, come what may.

Teresa and he had shared a sibling-like relationship, but if anybody understood the genial arm around the shoulder, it was them. There was that time when Teresa had been upset after falling out with Geoff over something trivial and he laid a genial arm around her shoulder. She turned to him, put both her arms in round each side of his jacket, massaging her hands lightly over his shirt as she cried. Geoff came upon them, took it a little too seriously and Teresa yelled, 'Bloody hell', stamped her foot a few times, 'Can't a man comfort a woman without expecting favours in return'. 'It looked very much to me that the woman was comforting the man'. Barry was almost certain it would have come to nothing, but who knows in a sensuous situation like that.

Patrick was on the phone when they stepped into the magnificent drawing room. "It's a boy, Uncle Liam! Seven pounds! I hear he has got his mother's good looks and my big feet".

Barry tensed: Why, the damned man had the bloody cheek to ring Uncle Tom Cobbley an' all.

Patrick replaced the phone, picked up the champagne and filled three glasses. "Only the best champagne on the market to wet my son's head; Dom Perignon 63; crisp, subtle and elegant".

Teresa held out her glass, "To little Patrick, may he grow up to be as wonderful as his father".

Patrick and she smiled knowingly at each other as they sipped the champagne. She then, with glass in hand, moved to the door, saying, "I'll leave you both to talk".

Barry never felt more in need of a stiff drink or going on the razzle but refused the champagne. "I don't particularly want to drink with you, O'Rafferty, for two reasons. Firstly: I have no cause to celebrate the birth of your child. Secondly: I need a clear head to say and do what I came for. I know your life revolves around booze and it wouldn't surprise me one damn bit if you befuddled her mind with it before you got your wicked way with her".

"I gave her the booze for medicinal purposes".

"So my hunch was right! You succeeded in lowering her inhibitions by rendering her incapable of rational decisions. How could you stoop so low, O'Rafferty? Why, it amounted to nothing short of date-rape! And from what Teresa has told me, you held on to get the last ounce of pleasure. What will happen when you meet her again? Has she whet your appetite for more?".

"I understand your rage, Barry. I would feel that way too if anyone did that to Jill, but you've got me all wrong: When I offered her the drink, the last thing on my mind was having it off with her; it just sort of evolved - we were both very vulnerable - each of us had given up completely on ever getting together again with either yourself or Teresa. Admittedly, the blame lay entirely with me, I was the instigator", but she was the more than willing consummator, such was the intensity of her pleasure that she was uncontrollable and wouldn't let go, it was she that needed that last ounce, "as for whetting my appetite for more - No! Christ No! Never!", well, not unless she.., "It was a one-off, never to be repeated. Did you ever find yourself in exceptional circumstances Barry wh..?".

"Mind your own bloody business - and keep away from my wife".

"That's not going to be easy as she is the mother of my child and I intend seeing my child every month - I wouldn't be so sure about her being your wife - you see, one can't be careful enough in this day and age so we had a discussion before we gave in to sex; I'm a safe sex man myself but was shocked by her disclosure that she was virtually a virgin. It could arguably have been the root cause of the break-up of your marriage".

Barry caught him by the scruff of the neck and raised his fist in fury - then let him go. If he hit the bugger's hard face he would break his knuckles and wouldn't be able to play the piano for weeks; also the bugger would know he wasn't very convincing at the strong-man act and would hit him back harder and he wasn't going to give him that satisfaction.

He turned on his heel in disgust. Patrick called after him, "Barry, perhaps I should tell you something!".

He stopped but didn't look back, "What now?".

"While I was having sex with Jill ..".

Barry turned around like a flash of lightening, every line of his face showing the depth and intensity of his savage feelings. He let loose an outburst of the most foul language imaginable; even Patrick couldn't have expressed such filth.

"For God's sake, man, calm down! I'm serious - hear me out - it could be of some consolation to you. While I was having se., sorry, making love to Jill, she ... ", he paused suspensively before continuing, "she called me Barry".

It was the sort of thing even Patrick O'Rafferty couldn't lie about. He had to believe it. "Thanks", he said, before letting himself out.

Patrick slurped the expensive champagne unsavourily as he looked daggers at the closed door and muttered under his breath, "She also told me she was very much in love with you - but a bastard who doesn't wet an innocent child's head doesn't deserve to be it's stepfather".

Barry fell deeper into despondency as he drove away from Checkerberry. The fact that she had whispered his name, in passion, to another man who was making love to her was of little or no consolation to him. He pulled into the first lay-by he came on, switched off the engine and unlike Patrick, felt no guilt as he racked himself with crying; there was no way his emotional torment could be kept pent-up any longer. The grief of losing her and the craving for her softness was gnawing away at him and had driven him to the pits of despair.

His mind was full of regretfulness as he relived his and her past mistakes. If only he had accepted that he loved her, as he undoubtedly did, from the very beginning, instead of pushing it aside; if only he had got his priorities right the day Teresa returned; if only she hadn't had the baby; if only she hadn't called him Patrick; if only the child wouldn't be a constant reminder of the liaison. If only ... if only ...

Chapter Twenty

"I can't believe it! I just can't believe it!".

"You'd better believe it". She smiled at him while handing over the precious bundle.

Patrick kissed the baby then held him out at arm's length in the airport arrival lounge and as every new parent before him, marvelled at the little miracle; he inspected him all over - ten tiny fingers, ten not so tiny toes, two tiny eyes, one tiny nose. "Has he got everything he should have underneath all this clutter of clothes you've put on him?".

"Everything". They laughed together with the amused spectators.

He handed him back to Jill then busied himself loading her luggage and pram on the trolley.

"Come with me, Bonny, those two woman will be talking babies till the cows come home".

Jane reached for the baby, it was her turn to make a fuss of him. "Now, that's your father's nose, I remember the shape well from the time of the wedding. I see he has your lovely eyes and Patrick's big feet".

"I've never seen Patrick's feet", said Jill laughing, "He kept his socks on".

Jane conveyed all the latest news; Michelle and Eamon

McGurkin had been married on Wednesday; Patrick and Teresa were excited about clinching a spectacular business deal with a large supermarket chain to supply them with four hundred cases of exclusive wine per week, bottled with the supermarket's own label in the Mosel by Karl Heinz. Then she surprised Jill by saying, "Tell Arthur, I've thought it over and I have decided to accept his invitation".

Jill looked at her quizzically, "Arthur? Do you mean my father?".

"Of course I mean your father! We were seated beside each other at the wedding and got on marvellously. Then when you were in the hospital, we spoke every day on the telephone. He told me about the beautiful area he lived in and how he would love me to see it".

Jill's spirits were slightly dampened - she didn't want to think of the wedding - not today; not any day.

"My father will like you, Jane, and do you know something? You will like him. He will treat you like a lady with old fashioned respect. I hope you become very good friends".

Jill and Teresa sat facing each other across the table in the room that had previously been the classroom, little Patrick lying contentedly on Jill's arm. It had been a big ordeal for them both to come together, each thinking they might not be acceptable to the other. Teresa had the added heartbreak of meeting up with Bonny again. They looked into each other's eyes intensely and smiled before Bonny ran off to play with the boys.

Jill watched as Teresa tried to quell her emotions and said, "Take it very easy, but when you get the chance, give her a big tight hug".

They shared an intuitive closeness due to their common knowledge and experiences; being as extensively familiar with the individual personality of each child as they were with each other's husband.

"Patrick and I do have our differences, but we agree to differ. I'm afraid I also have to be the taskmaster where the children are concerned as Patrick is so easy-going". She became pensive, "I love him very much but there are times when his ways and manners creep through to the children".

As she spoke Bonny was cautiously sidling up to Alan who was engrossed in his computer.

"What sort of game is that?", she asked.

"It's my new computer game".

"Can I play?".

"N O spells no, little girl".

"Why? I want to play".

"Because only one person can play at a time", he said

getting agitated.

"Then we could play in turns", said Bonny hopefully.

"No! Shove off!".

Bonny was downcast as she moved off. Teresa was mortified and half rose from her chair but Jill gestured for her not to interfere.

"Oh, alright then", said Alan as he watched her go.
"This is what you do, Bonny ...".

Jill smiled at Teresa. "You know something - Patrick O'Rafferty, for all his rough and ready ways, is kind and open and would never hurt anyone and that's getting through to the children".

Teresa laughed and told Jill the story of the day he visited the Head Office in London and even chatted up Miss Foster. They were in stitches when Patrick and Jamie came in. "I sure as hell hope you two woman aren't exchanging notes on my techniques", to which they laughed even louder.

Patrick tickled the baby on the cheek and spoke in gobbledegook, "Goochie.. goochie.. goochie..".

Jamie sidled over to Teresa and whispered in her ear. A fleeting pang of jealousy shot through Jill. Being shy, once upon a time, it would have been her ear he would have whispered in.

"Jill", Teresa said, with her arm around him, "Jamie wants to know if you would listen to his new pieces on the flute?".

The fleeting pang of jealousy was quickly overtaken by the delightful feeling of unity with him, "There is nothing I would like more". She stood up and laid the baby on Patrick's shoulder, then held out her hand to Jamie, but he was too excited to see it as he charged ahead of her to the music room.

Chapter Twenty one

Jill's father picked them up at the airport. She was amused at his complaining about the amount of stuff she had. "Do modern babies really need all this for one weekend? When you were small we took less on a month's holiday".

"Things are different now, Father".

"You can say that again", he said in a disgruntled manner, "You could have kept your good husband if you hadn't put yourself about".

She bit her lip - Ah, well, it had to come sometime.

When they eventually got settled into the house, Bonny was giving her Grandpa a blow-by-blow account of the weekend when she noticed the letter. She reached up and took it in her hands - turning it over, her heart fell; it was the Solicitor's letter she had been dreading.

She went to her bedroom, sat on the bed and tore it open hastily. Inside were two letters: She read the Decree Absolute and her heart broke. Her eyes scanned the other letter and getting to the amount of her settlement she couldn't read the figure, her eyes were too blurred with tears. There were a lot of noughts and she knew that she and the children would be able to live in luxury for the rest of their lives. She threw herself on top of the bed and cried her heart out - the noughts meant nothing to her except perhaps the true meaning of the word: zero, infinitely nothing, non-existent, null and void.

* * *

The letter lay on top of the piano, aside from the rest that were accumulating fast. His long slim fingers played a melancholy tune as if his world was collapsing in pieces around him.

If it hadn't been for Miki's perseverance while taking the full force of his filthy infuriating anger, he probably would have been dead by now. He had spent days on end sitting in a darkened room getting himself so drunk he was unable to drag himself to bed. If he wasn't throwing booze into himself he was throwing it up. Meg, his housekeeper, hadn't the stomach to put up with his filthy ways so he told her to bugger off out of his sight and leave him alone to wallow. Miki continued to come round each morning mostly to find him lying on the goatskin rug like a dog, very often clutching some item of her clothing wrapped around an empty vodka bottle. The bottle was his only sustenance and he would have stumbled for it straight away first thing in the morning; didn't want to eat and when Miki tried to swap the booze for milk he called him a filthy swine and worse while raking up old skeletons.

Swearing and throwing abuse at Miki had been the limit of his vocabulary together with the heartsore cries, "Ji-ill, Ji-ill..."

Against all the odds Miki stayed loyal, never showed as if he was losing patience although there must have been times he felt like throttling him, and with perpetual chiding he effectively helped him claw his way out of the pit and onto the piano stool to play again, albeit lamentably.

The piano keys, slowly but surely, superseded the drink. He needed to play now as obsessively as he had needed the bottle a month previously; in his despair it became his instrument of self expression: Grief, hate, fear and hope.

There was only one woman who could get his life out of this state of disorder, inspire him to compose and play again in public, but she was the mother of Patrick O'Rafferty's child.

As he thought of her he seemed to plunge even further into gloom, his fingers producing a sensual melodic grace as they stole over the piano.

He thought of the night she had inspired him to reach his peak performance by surpassing his own expectations, at the Corn Exchange in Cambridge. The audience were entranced as he captured the agony and ecstasy of love in his music and could never have guessed he was playing for one woman only, his blood flowing fast through his veins in a desperate need of her. The fact that she was in the audience, her eyes never leaving him for a moment, had caused him to submit a symphonic plea, an intensely personal piece, to melt a lover's heart. When he bowed at the end, the crowd screaming for more, he had eyes only for her as he peered into the dimness of the auditorium.

When they got home her glance held his just a little longer

than usual as she said goodnight, then retired to her room. He poured himself another drink, taking his time over it, as he tried to fathom that intriguing look. He threw the last of the whisky into the back of his throat and went to her.

As he stood and looked down on her sleeping form the memory of her beautiful glowing face in the aftermath of their night of love came to haunt him and in bleak despair his heart broke for the way he had treated her. All she had wanted was his love and he had, in his insensitivity, thrown it back in her face; she had no feelings left for him other than being the father of the children she loved. The gaze had been misinterpreted; she had recognised in the music his need of her and had been sorry for him, but was paying him back in kind.

The telephone rang. He continued to play, the music evoking a mood tinged with regret. It rang continually with no letting up before he rose from the stool to answer it.

"Hello, Barry. I've added two notes on the third line of the song you thought about dedicating to Jill. Dr Thorpe and Miki Delecour are ready to take the pop world by storm". He let loose a hearty laugh before starting to sing: "I've never needed anyone
Never needed anyone
Never needed anyone", he dropped his voice a note and vibrated a long drawn out, "..so b-a-d".

Barry slammed down the phone. He walked to the window and looked out over the gardens, deep in thought.

Miki was right he needed her badly; without her he might just as well have been left to drink himself to death. It was eight months now since he had confronted Patrick O'Rafferty and every single day since, whether he be drunk or sober, he thought of his words, albeit in the crude context, 'She called me Barry'. Had she, in the end, grown to love him, and what were her feelings for O'Rafferty? Without doubt O'Rafferty loved Teresa but was he the type to allow himself an element of diversity? The mind-boggler had tormented him for months, but it was at last beginning to bother him less. His craving for her was such that he would be willing to share - even with Patrick O'Rafferty.

He turned and went to the piano, picked up the letter and read it again.

Dear Dr Thorpe,
As you are probably aware, your daughter, Bonny, is a pupil at our school. We are tremendously excited that she has inherited the remarkable quality of her mother's singing voice. She deserves someone with your masterly musical stimulus and creativity to devise a programme excellent enough to present her voice to its best advantage. She ...

He folded the letter in haste, made one phone call to the holiday agency, then rushed through the house throwing items haphazardly into a suitcase. "All right, Miki, kill or cure, I'll give it a whirl".

He made his way to the furthermost tip of Devon; this part of the country seemed so far removed from the rest, it was almost as if he was entering another world. At last he drove along the winding narrow country lane to the thatched cottage and parked his car in front of the little rackety gate. It was spring-time and the gardens were neat and tidy, different coloured daisies and daffodils in little clumps on the lawn.

After he had deposited his luggage he walked up the road where below the golden stretches of sand seemed to ripple in the sunshine and the sound of the waves filling his ears; his step quickening as he neared her cottage.

She stood before him agog, her light blue eyes wide, stunning him with her exceptional good looks. Her naturally pink lips slightly open in amazement. She had the most kissable soft lips imaginable and how he could have avoided them for so long was beyond comprehension. Her long blond hair hung neatly on her shoulders, the pendant he had given her lay loosely between her breasts on a gold chain. He managed to get the words out at last. "I have been asked by Mrs Thompson of the Bebe school to compose a theme for their May-day concert and I was wondering if I may have a loan of a little girl with long black hair and a little boy with big feet, in your surveillance, of course, and dammit, Jill, I've never needed anyone so bad?".

The tears started to roll down her cheeks. Never in her wildest dreams could she have imagined him to be other than stylish, distinctive and oozing class. This fuzzy faced, unkempt man standing before her, lines deeply etched around his eyes, in crumpled clothing, was devoid of his usual confident showy exterior. To see him like this almost drove her mad with desire. She wanted to put her arms out to him straight away, draw him to her and smother the most grizzly, unruly, flecked with grey, beard she had ever seen with kisses.

Her voice wavered as she chose her words carefully, "I'm sorry Mr ... I don't hire out children, but I might make an exception if you would consider taking them on for good, in my surveillance, of course, and Oh, Barry, I've never needed anyone so bad either".

He pushed her through the open door before taking her in his arms and locking her tight against him as he kissed her tears away. He then sought her lips with his in a long, passionate and intense way that erased all their doubts. "I love you, my darling, and I always have from the very first moment I set eyes on you. Now that I have a clear understanding of my priorities, will you marry me - again?".

She pressed her cheek against his and in a daze her shining eyes ascended to the smiling picture of her mother on the wall. Had all the long months of gloom and doom lifted? Was it possible that the sun would peep through?.

"Damn you, it goes against my grain to give in to a man so cock sure of himself and I do love you so much, but before I can commit myself I have to be absolutely sure that every time you look at my child, you won't see Patrick".

He looked down on the sleeping child and said, "I never fulfilled my purpose when I went to see that bugger. I intended knocking him flat for lying through his bloody Irish teeth".

She compulsively released herself from his grip and dropped her eyes. "That's it then! We can't ever get together", she said in despair.

When her eyes eventually came up to meet his, he was smiling. "I have an innate love for children regardless of who they are fathered by and I swear I shall never look at him and see Patrick. Did you ever look at my children and see Teresa?".

"No, Barry! Never", she smiled before continuing, "But then, I didn't know Teresa".

He ventured cautiously, "I know Patrick O'Rafferty has a deep love for Teresa and I hope I am right in being assured of yours, but I can't help worrying that if you and he ...".

She pressed her fingers firmly over his lips silencing him. "Barry, I love you more than anything in the world. I admit Patrick and I have become closer but that is only because he is the father of my child. I swear to you, it was a one-off, never to be repeated".

"Where's your father and Bonny?", he mumbled wildly in her ear as he gathered her to him.

"They've gone to Aunt Alice's house for tea".

"Do you think there would be time..?".

She held him to her as if fuelled with a wild delirium, "There wouldn't be if I wanted to have you scrupulously, squeaky clean by scrubbing you all over in the bath and getting rid of that scruffy, grizzly beard, but you're in luck, I don't want that, I'll have you as you are - I've always had a hankering to go to bed with a long grimy haired hippy".

His mouth was just about to come down on hers when a sudden thought went through his mind. He went to the pram and lowered the quilt to reveal little Patrick's infamous big feet and picking one up kissed it tenderly, then eased the bottle from the sleeping child's mouth.

Jill screamed and wrestled with him as he sprinkled the black current juice all over her immaculate clean clothes and shining hair. "You can't have it all your way, I've had a hankering too you know".

Grabbing a handful of her sticky messy hair, he dragged her to the bedroom amid the warm glow of laughter. Perhaps Patrick O'Rafferty had indirectly taught him that life was too short to be lonely or serious and that laughter was the main flavour of love.

Their clothes went flying in all directions and just as he dragged the last item from her body, he looked at her red-bloodedly, his eyes twinkling, and she was certain he was going to utter something very sexy, when he said, "Footballer's feet indeed! Rudolf Nureyev had feet like that. I intend moulding Patrick O'Rafferty's son into a ballet dancer".